PROTECT
WHAT'S
YOURS

FU ABDUL SA'EED

WRITERS REPUBLIC L.L.C.
515 Summit Ave. Unit R1
Union City, NJ 07087, USA

Website: *www.writersrepublic.com*
Hotline: *1-877-656-6838*
Email: *info@writersrepublic.com*

Ordering Information:
Quantity sales. Special discounts are available on quantity purchases by corporations, associations, and others. For details, contact the publisher at the address above.

Library of Congress Control Number:		2022905808	
ISBN-13:	978-1-63728-984-6	[Paperback Edition]
	978-1-64620-997-2	[Hardback Edition]
	978-1-63728-985-3	[Digital Edition]

Rev. date: 08/21/2022

ACKNOWLEDGMENT

First, I would like to give all praise to Allah (SWT) for guiding me down a diff erent path. Without Him, there would be no me: therefore no entertainment for the masses.

ALLAHU AKBAR!

To my pretty girl, Danazia Nicole, what more can I ask for in a daughter? When all else fails, you keep me going with your interesting, witty, and yet complex way of thinking and not to mention the whole dark comedian thing. . . I love you little one, and thank you for accepting me for who I am and not who the world portrays me to be.

For my little homie, my son Davon, I know that life has tossed a lot of shit in the game as far as us, but never think for a moment that I didn't love you. This prison situation just has always stood in our way, but things will get better and my smaller lil baby homies will always have a "G" of a pop pop! FACTS!

My cousin Keisha, I love you kid and I know that at times I could be a pain in the ass, but you always remain there for me with no complaints EVER! No matter how busy you are, and we all know how that full your life is, you always do everything that I ask with no hesitation. I always call you my secretary and for years you have worked for free, but know that when this project takes off, I GOT YOU KID! Thank you for all of your support and for always pushing me to get this out. I truly do and forever will appreciate you, cousin-sincerely speaking.

Big shout out for my cousin, Ant. Always popping shit but always there, every call answered even when you are at fake work, (real work but we both know that you don't do shit). Love is love and family is everything, you once told me that, and the mental support that you give overrides the money any day. Also thanks for finding these pictures for the front and back of this book, I guess graphic design goes to you.

To my Aunt Bridget. . . What can I say but I love your crazy old ass. You are out of commission due to your injury, but Insha-Allah, I will be able to help you out a little. I OWE YOU THE WORLD. You have always been there for me, no matter how much of a problem that I was you and the big homie, (Uncle Junie), always had that door open for me. THANK YOU FOREVER!

To my brothers… Spank, Sudan, and Will… twenty plus years of friendship/brotherhood. We have been through a lot over the years but still remain loyal on top of everything else. I love yall for the sake of Allah. Never forget that Line of Respect. Dulla you know what I'm talking about. My cousin Tasha, I did it kid. Lil cousin Ebony, I have always loved you like a sister and I thank you for always rocking out with me, even though you are still mad at me. I love you and again I apologize for breaking my word to you. I'll be home soon enough. And Aunt Carla, I can't forget about you… All that I could possibly say is…HOMIE, HOMIE…you used to kick these prison doors down every week before the accident, no matter where they put me, you was putting miles on that car every single weekend. I love you Auntie and I thank you.

To my mother Symone, and siblings, I love you all. And Rest in peace to O.G. Butch…

Shout out to all of the real ones behind these walls Abby (my co-D) we stood firm together and it's almost over, Rozay a.k.a. Roger that, yeah I gave you a part, this prison shit is just a stepping stone. Najee, Slay, Bino, Lights, O, my boy Ish, and all the brothers, and all the brothers that I may have missed, big love to the ones that were always genuine.

Also shout out to Zay Muh a.k.a Meanie for giving me a good review during the process of me writing this. I remember you saying, "If it's whack Imma tell you!" instead you came back with that face and nod of approval.

Now to my beautiful amazing spouse…Chicky you are hard to describe, but the best feeling that I get is with you, thank you for accepting this life and I know it could be hard at times with the time and all, but I promise to always make it easy as possible on. Your loyalty is spectacular and many women doesn't possess that, especially when it comes to prison love, but you got it… and I am forever grateful to have and come home to you. I love you for the sake of Allah, and I thank you for your patience. Oh, and shout out to all of my real niggas, and shout out to all of my fake niggas for making us real niggas look so good. And to all of you hating ass niggas, stay stagnated and out of my way, and watch this process. Maybe yall will learn something. SERIOUSLY!

A.C. (Atlantic City) stand up. We out here.

BIG SHOUT OUT TO MY NIGGA PATTERSON FUZZ, MUSCLE TEAM UP, EVERYBODY EAT, YOU KNOW THE MOVEMENT… I see you my wardy, and I'm always on board with the squad, get with it…

I can't forget two amazing people, T and P, both of you get me through these days with such graceful images, I appreciate both of your presence.

Fu Abdul-Sa'eed

INCARCERATED ME

Closed in and captivated by the mindset that I have discovered within myself.

I am a gentleman amongst women but a true gangsta on the surface in every aspect of the term. This is the life inside of the mind of an incarcerated me.

Living in a world outside of the life that I will continue to live in as I climb the highest depths of my mind. A place where I am free beyond these prison walls, a place where I will continue to dream.

Physically gravitated by steel cased in concrete, with steel locks on doors. But somehow my mind has found ways to escape this mental nightmare that my body will be forced to endure.

Mentally I am elevated in the distance! And I have found my calling facilitating a change in the mindsets of people who view guys such as myself as monsters—who view us more as society's menaces instead of the incarcerated versions of themselves.

This is the life inside of the mind of an incarcerated me.

CHAPTER

1

Present day

Silence sat alone in his cell, thinking about the mistake he made that landed him in prison for the next 185 years. He only has a few years into the stretch and, at times, it took a toll on him, especially after seeing his wife and daughter. Despite the time he has, and what he has put her through, she is there for him no matter what, driving well over a hundred miles every weekend for a three-hour visit.

He was a good man to his wife and an even better father to their daughter, but he had a dark side that neither of them ever saw. Growing up, he never had a family, only leaning on his best friend—and partner to most of his crimes—so it is safe to say that the streets truly did raise him, or rather he raised hell in the streets.

As he looked at his photos, he started to replay all the murders he has executed. If only he had murdered the link that put him in prison, he'd still be a free man. But he broke his one cardinal rule—"No loose ends"—which is a regret he will have to live with while serving his time.

Silence has made a lot of money in the murder game, and his name was heavy in the underworld, only spoken amongst the city's biggest drug lords. Even then he was only referred to as the "Reaper."

His mother gave him the name Silence because of the fact that he never cried as a baby.

Silence Jihad. A born killer.

Since birth, he has never been one for too many words, only speaking when spoken to or when he has something to say. And even then that is not too often.

—ɯɯ—

"Si, I just got off the phone with Rican, and he finally got the official word about that fuck boy from up top," Spizz said as he walked into the cell, interrupting Silence's thought process.

Silence and Spizz have been friends—well, more like brothers—since the third grade. They grew up together in Pitney, a housing project in the downtown area of Atlantic City, and are also co-defendants serving their time together at the New Jersey State Prison in Trenton, N.J.

Their love for each other is genuine and both will do just about anything for one another.

They met this cat named B-Boy not long before they were arrested and came to find out he was the one somehow responsible for their incarceration. Silence vowed to get his revenge one way or another. But after they were arrested, B-Boy went into hiding and nobody knew where he was.

Until now.

"Tell me what you know," Silence responded with a look of death in his eyes. He replayed the night when he and Spizz were arrested for the murder of two FBI informants and one of their families.

Four-and-a-half years before their arrest

Silence and Spizz waited patiently inside a townhouse in Hoboken, New Jersey, for their target.

This was pretty much a regular day for these men. Silence enjoyed every second of inflicting pain on others.

"Ticktock . . . ticktock," Silence repeated in a serious tone as he and Spizz continue their wait.

Spizz walked away from the window he was looking out of and headed towards the man's four-year-old daughter, who was lying on her side, bound and gagged next to her decapitated mother.

"Damn, baby girl, where is your daddy? He should be here tucking you in and kissing you good night," he said, leaning over her while moving the hair over her face.

Next to the little girl sat her older brother, who was home from college for Christmas break, also bound but not gagged.

"Leave my sister alone," the young man said.

Spizz looked over and smiled before cracking him in his mouth with the butt of his gun.

"Keep ya mouth shut youngin."

The force from the hit was enough to knock the kid out. As he lay there bleeding with his jaw apparently broken, Spizz stood up and walked back over to the window to see if he saw anybody pulling up.

"Silence, where the fuck is this nigga?" Spizz asked very impatiently as he peeked through the blinds. "We have been in this crib for far too long."

Silence sat stoned-faced on the edge of the coffee table, ignoring the question altogether, continuing his rant . . .

"Tick . . . tock . . ."

Then BOC . . . BOC!!!

He shot the young boy twice—once to the head and the other to the heart.

"Patience," he said calmly as he lit another blunt.

A few minutes later, a car could be heard driving over the gravel in the driveway. Spizz slightly moved the blind as to where he could see without being seen to be sure it was indeed the man they were waiting for.

"About fucking time," Spizz whispered, relieved of his frustration from the waiting game.

Silence shifted his body on the coffee table so that he could be facing the door once the man entered, while Spizz stood behind it.

As the man undid the locks and walked into his home, the first image he saw was a man sitting on his table.

"What the fuck?" he said as he attempted to reach for the gun he had tucked in his waistband.

"Wrong thing to do, don't you think?" Spizz asked, his gun pointed at the back of the man's head as he closed the door behind him.

The man stood there, confused, as his eyes scanned the room. He could not believe what he was seeing. He covered his nose from the strong weed smoke mixed with the smell of the bowel movements released during the murders.

There lay his son's lifeless body, along with his wife lying there with her head cut off. His daughter was bound and gagged, lying on her side in a pool of her mother's blood.

"Have a seat," Silence said to the man. "This will be over in a matter of minutes."

The unknown man slowly walked over and sat on the couch right in front of the table where Silence was sitting.

"You do not look afraid. Usually in a situation like the one you are in, one would beg for his life, offer money, or try to attempt something very foolish," Silence said with a slight grin on his face.

The man, unable to answer right away, began to shake uncontrollably, as the reality of what was happening started to sink in. Frantically he looked back and forth from Silence to his daughter, the only one left of his family before speaking.

"What do you want? Money?" the man stuttered, hoping they would leave if he gave them what they wanted.

"Nah, personally I don't care for what you have to offer. I'm here for your life . . . Nothing more," Silence replied. "But first, you'll watch your daughter die."

Seeing his opportunity to get what he came for, Spizz walked over to their victim and pointed his .44 mag at the man's face.

"He didn't come for the money, but I did," Spizz said while moving closer to man, so they could be face to face.

"So y'all are going to kill me and my daughter and still take my fucking money? Fuck both of y'all niggas. Do what you do, but I'm not giving up shit," yelled the victim before spitting in Silence's face.

At this point, the man's fear went out the window. Knowing you will die anyway can do that to you.

"Brave man," Silence said while wiping the spit from his left eye.
CRACK!

"Ah shit!" the man screamed in agony after Spizz pistol-whipped him.

"I like you. You have heart, but it is too bad you pissed off the wrong people," Spizz told the man. "Now, where is the money, and where is the work?"

The man sat there quietly, blood dripping down the side of his face, with a look that would put fear in any man. But Silence and Spizz were not just any man.

"I tell you what. Tell us where everything is and you have my word that I will let your daughter live," Spizz continued.

"Tick . . . tock!" Silence repeated as he approached the little girl. She could be heard trying to scream despite being gagged, so all that could be heard was a slight muffle.

"So what will be that pretty little girl's future, my man? Does she live or die with the rest of you?" Spizz asked, looking dead at their victim with no sense of emotion nor remorse.

"Please leave her alone," the man begged as he helplessly watched Silence lean in and pick up his daughter, the only one that could possibly be left of his family.

"Tick . . . Tock," Silence continued as he wrapped his hands around the little girl's neck.

"Please, not my baby girl. I'll tell you everything, please just put her down," the man cried out.

Hearing this, Silence put the child down and sat back on the table. Spizz got the information he came for.

"I got a safe in my daughter's room behind her dresser," the man said, putting his head down, relieved that these men would at least spare his daughter. "It's also a few bricks down in the basement."

"What is the combination?" Spizz asked as he pulled out his cell phone to type it in so he would not to forget it once he is upstairs.

"Twenty-seven, thirty-two, forty-eight," the man answered.

Silence pulled his weapon and pointed it at the man. Spizz went upstairs to retrieve what could possibly be in the safe.

Upstairs, Spizz found the little girl's room, which wasn't hard at all. The room door had big pink letters that spelled "Aminah."

Entering the room, Spizz noticed the dresser the man could be speaking about. He went over to move it to the side.

"Jackpot," Spizz said to himself as he pulled his cell phone out to look at the combination. He typed it into to the safe's keyboard. Click. It opened.

He then scanned the room for something to put the money in and settled for a pink unicorn book bag hanging from the door knob of the closet sitting right beside the dresser.

Back downstairs, Silence waited patiently for his accomplice to come with his reward.

"Who sent you?" the man asked, but Silence ignored him.

Before the man got a chance to say anything else, Spizz appeared back downstairs with the book bag filled with the contents of the safe.

"One more stop," Spizz said as he headed towards the basement.

"Where?" he asked the man, stopping dead in his tracks as he remembered that he never got the exact location of the kilos of heroin that was supposed to be in the basement.

"Inside the washing machine," the man answered in a very defeated voice.

Spizz went to the basement. He came back shortly after with another bag filled with four kilos heroin.

Silence noticed his friend and asked, "Satisfied?"

Spizz shook his head "yes" as he went over and dropped the bags by the front door.

Silence then stood up. He walked back over to the little girl and shot her in the head. The man got up screaming and tried the rush Silence but was forcefully stopped by Spizz with a gun butt to the back of his head.

"You said you would let my daughter live," the man cried out.

"I said that I would. I never said that he would," Spizz said, pointing at Silence.

The man buckled and started to sob uncontrollably, yelling helpless rants about killing the men and calling them heartless and how he would see them in hell.

Silence stood up, smiled, and walked over to the man. Before shooting him twice in the head, he said, "GOD sent me," answering the dead man's question about who sent him.

"Come on, my nigga, we out," Spizz yelled to Silence as they walked out the door. "Five bodies in one night. Shit gone be hot for a while, brah," he said to his friend.

"Indeed. Now take me to collect my money. And make that count six for tonight," Silence said as they drove away from their recent crime scene.

"Nah, brah. B-Boy good for the moment. I got plans with son," Spizz said, hoping that this one time he will get things his way.

Silence looked at his friend and said very firmly, "Make these plans quick. Rules are set in place for a reason."

Silence has never liked B-Boy. It was just something about son that didn't quite sit right with him, but he played it cool for business's sake.

Spizz, on the other hand, has always been a man of reason, always willing to give a nigga a shot, so Silence played along . . . for the moment. But will it cost him everything.

CHAPTER

2

Sixteen years earlier, summer of '99

"Welcome home, my nigga," Spizz greeted his right-hand man, who had just been released from the juvenile detention center. "Shit been crazy these past few months that you been gone, kid. Niggas making wild noise; especially when they heard you beat that homi," Spizz continued, glad to have his goon back on the streets.

"Where's my gun?" Silence asked calmly, waiting to be reunited with his steady companion.

"Damn. No love? First thing ya mind is putting in work, huh? What the fuck, my nigga. Just chill for a few." Spizz attempted to reason with this ill-tempered friend.

This is what he was always afraid of. He hasn't quite embraced the fact that his brother from another has a different way of thinking and doing things than most cats their age.

Both fourteen years old, the two friends grew up in the slum of the slums. From early on, they knew what they had to do to survive—and that was the life of crime.

Spizz was the one who would rather flip a pack, and maybe rob a nigga here and there, as a means to live comfortably at that young age.

Silence, on the other hand, was a killer. Before being released, he went to juvee for killing some old head cat around the projects. The story goes that this dude was on some bullshit about his man Spizz taking all of his flow, so he spoke up and told Spizz that he couldn't hustle around there anymore.

Silence heard this and blew the ol' boy's head off in front of the whole projects. He was zero tolerance when it came to his family and the dudes he fucked with, which wasn't many. The case was dismissed due to a lack of evidence—and it didn't hurt that the only one who came forward ended up as a missing person report.

"You know where my love is—with you, my nigga—but shit has to be done before I can just chill and sit back. Now where is my strap?" Silence responded coldly.

Frustrated with his brother's attitude, Spizz hands him the blue steel .357 he brought just days before Silence was released.

"So, what's the plan, kid?" asked Spizz, already knowing what was next.

"We wait, then we take over," Silence said before sparking the blunt that Spizz brought with him for the drive back to the hood.

—∭—

Back in the hood, the whole projects welcomed Silence. Old heads looked at him on an equal level, and all the old head bitches wanted to fuck. Which was regular when it comes to hood stars, no matter the age, but none of this fazed Silence because he was more focused on revenge.

"Welcome home, nephew," Muhmit said as he approached Silence with open arms.

Muhmit was Silence's mom's brother, and a stickup boy at heart. He loved his nephew something fierce.

"What up, Mu? I heard about the situation that damn near wiped you out. How the fuck did you let them niggas catch you off guard like that?" Silence asked his uncle, who got hit up a few times the night he got bagged.

"Fucking with that stupid bitch, Toya, had me drunk as shit out here," Muhmit replied, not knowing that his answer just signed her death certificate.

Hearing what he already knew, just wanting to confirm it, Silence cut the conversation short.

"Unc, I'ma holla at you later. I gotta take care of some business, but we definitely going gone kick it about that situation," Silence said before going his separate way from everyone else, including Spizz.

Silence has one thing on his mind, and that is murder. He doesn't let anything go. Whether it happened to him or someone close to him, he seeks revenge. Leaving it alone is a sure sign of weakness.

Later that night Silence leaned up in a fiend's whip that he rented earlier that day. He's been sitting in the same spot, smoking blunt after blunt, waiting for the nigga, Blaze, to come through, so he could handle what needed to be done. Silence waited patiently parked in the alley on the side of Blaze's crib.

A few minutes later, he saw a car pulling up in front of the house. He got off his parked car and started to walk over to where the car was pulling up.

As Blaze got out of his gold Acura, he was startled by Silence's presence.

"Oh, shit. What's good, lil brah? I didn't even see creeping. I heard that you was out but didn't know when," Blaze stuttered.

Blaze was some in the way ass nigga that does shit just to fit in, and word was that he was the one that hit Muhmit the night Silence got booked for the body. He was supposed to hit the nigga Cheeese, some rat-ass nigga who got Blaze's brother fifteen years for a robbery and missed bitting Muhmit six times.

Before Blaze could say anything else, he was met with six bullets to his face. Neighbors and the people outside started to scream and run for cover as the body slid down the side of the car.

Silence walked back to the alley where he was parked as if nothing ever happened. Once inside the car, he lit another blunt.

He said to himself, "One down, one to go."

Pulling out of the alley, he lit the corner heading back to the hood to his next target.

Knock, knock!

Silence stood on the porch, waiting patiently for someone to open the door.

"Who is it?" a female voice yelled out. He didn't bother to answer, causing the woman on the other side of the door to become angry and swing it open violently.

"I said, who the fuck is . . . Oh, hey, Silence. You looking for Muhmit?" Toya asked when she saw him standing there with the biggest smile.

"Nah, I'm here for you," Silence said, still somewhat smiling.

"Oh, what can I do for you, baby?" Toya asked, confused as to what Silence could possibly want with her.

Toya was the typical project whore and was known for setting niggas up, but for some reason his uncle loved her to death. Maybe it was that fat ass and the head game that everybody talked about. Whatever it was, Muhmit was whipped.

"Ya life!" Silence answered before shooting her in the head.

As months went on, he started going to all of the city dope boys, offering his service of murder to anybody who needed them, and through time calls started coming in.

Ten years later, winter of '09

Over the past few years, a lot of bodies have dropped in and around the city they called home. Outsiders looked at Atlantic City as a gambling and tourist spot, but beyond those lights there was darkness and an evil presence that was felt throughout the city. Hood to hood, niggas came together to get rid of these two evil forces.

"Yo, son, that nigga Si be creeping me the fuck out," Dutch said to Bullet as they were sitting at the table, bagging up work in one of the trap spots on the MaVa strip.

"I feel you kid, but his man Spizz got the best work in the city, and I don't see us going against that. At least not now," Bullet replied.

"You think that nigga is going to be with son when he comes through for that bread?" Dutch asked, hoping he would not be in the presence of Silence.

11

"Stop being so fucking paranoid all the time. We haven't done nothing to brah that would put us on his bad side, so we good. Besides, don't the nigga fuck with ya sister?"

Silence and Tisha have been together since the beginning of time and they have a four-year-old daughter together. That is how her little brother, Dutch, got involved with Spizz on the drug tip.

Silence and Dutch have never had too many conversations. Dutch was always a little wary of Silence. Silence was not one to hold pointless conversations anyway, so the lack of communication between the two didn't bother him.

For a few years, Silence watched lil Dutch getting to a dollar and Spizz peeped it, too. When Silence killed Dutch's connect, Spizz stepped in, seeing potential in the youngin. He eventually took him under his wing.

Spizz liked the lil nigga. In fact, he had the kind of love for him that an older brother would have.

Dutch and Bullet are from the other side of town. Their block has a lot of beef with the young boys where Silence and Spizz were from, but Dutch and Bullet stayed in their lane and never got involved. They were more so into getting money while staying away from the violence that came along with it.

"Yeah, he do, but from what I hear, the nigga is only loyal to his hood. Shit, he fuck around and kill Tish over some bullshit one day," Dutch said, serious as hell about the comment he just made.

"Chill the fuck out, so we can finish this shit, my nigga. I'm telling you, we good. He just quiet as fuck, but we good," Bullet said, still frustrated with his boy's paranoia.

KNOCK.

"That should be brah right there," Bullet said, getting up to open the door.

"Hold up, let me grab my strap. I told you the nigga creep me the fuck out," Dutch said as he got his gun from under the couch.

Bullet looked through the peephole and saw that it was indeed Silence, so he opened the door to let him in. "What's good, big brah?"

Before Bullet could extend his arm to embrace his mentor's right-hand man, he was met with two shots to his head.

12

Silence then focused his attention on Dutch, stepping over Bullet's body as he entered the house.

Scared and traumatized by what had just taken place, Dutch was unable to move.

He tried to speak, but couldn't, then BOC!

Silence shot him in the head, causing his body to fly into the table, flipping the money and drugs all over place while he twitched, hanging on to life.

Putting him out of his misery, Silence walked to where he was lying, stood over him, and shot him twice in the head.

He then left without a word, leaving behind the money he came for. Once outside the apartment he lit a blunt and hopped behind the wheel. He headed toward his next location, which was uptown, to meet one of his most trusted young boys. On the drive there he received a call from a cat named Reach that he'd been trying to get with for quite some time.

Reach pretty much ran North Philly, but he lacked that killer instinct. Getting more to the point, son was a bitch nigga in power, with a lot of paper to throw around. We all know that story well.

Silence was parked on Broad and Market, kicking it with some lil bitch when Reach pulled up. He had this silly-ass look on his face, like him and Silence went way back or something.

Silence knew exactly who son was; in fact, he was there hoping to bump into the clown. Everybody who was supposed to know what it was with Silence did, and that was most millionaire cats like Reach. When they met, numbers were exchanged and it was only a matter of time before the nigga reached out.

The phone rang twice before Silence picked up.

"What up?" Silence asked nonchalantly.

"My nigga, I need you out this way; I got some real serious issues that I want you to look into," Reach said in a real serious tone. "When can you make it out this way?"

"Whenever is most convenient for you," Silence replied, somewhat dazed thinking about his next method of murder and the payday that comes with his passion.

"Shit urgent. Can you come through tonight?" Reach pushed, sounding like whatever the situation maybe was really hurting his pockets, or it was the fear from the pressure being put on him.

Either way, Silence senses this and will use it as a means for a much more expensive ticket.

"Cool. Let me hit my brah. But first, let me know where we meeting you at?" Silence asked, hoping this scary-ass nigga would not to want to meet all in public.

"Come to my crib. I'll text you the address, " Reach said before hanging up, glad to have his problems close to being solved.

"Stupid-ass nigga," Silence said while smiling to himself. He continued on his drive to meet his youngin.

As he pulled up on the block, he noticed young Aido posted up amongst his lil squad that he referred to as "THE FAMILY."

Seeing his mentor, Aido ran over and hopped in the passenger side. "What up my-G?" he asked Silence as he closed the car door behind him. Aido couldn't help but admire the black leather interior of Silence's smoke-gray Range Rover. "Damn, I got to get me one of these shits."

"One day," was Silence's only response.

He took a liking to young Aido, who reminded him of a little him, even though they were only a few years apart.

"What did you say this nigga name was that was out here asking about me?" Silence asked his youngin.

"Oh, yeah. They call son B-Boy. This nigga that I fucks with ran into son at the Taj, and he mentioned ya name," Aido replied. "My young boy said he drive a white Beemer, with New York tags."

Silence sat back and thought for a minute before speaking again. "Find out everything you can about this nigga, and fast. Understood?" Silence said very calmly, not worried much about the situation.

"You want him dead?" asked young Aido, ready to prove his loyalty to his big brah.

Silence looked at his youngin and smiled, glad to have such loyal companions at his side. "Nah, just information for now."

Going their separate ways, Silence drove off contemplating his next job as he pulled out his cell phone to call Spizz.

"What up, my goon?" Spizz asked as he answered on the first ring.

"Meet me in the hood. We gotta got to Philly tonight," Silence said into the receiver.

"I'm leaving Delaware now. I'll be there in an hour." Spizz replied, ending the call.

He knew what time it was, and looked forward to what he would come out with when it was all said and done. Although he couldn't stomach the murder, he always was down to ride with his brother.

"Next stop, Philly," Spizz said to himself out loud as he pushed his CLS 550 up the pike.

CHAPTER

3

That night . . .

On their way to Philly, Spizz received a call telling him that somebody had just killed Bullet at their spot on the back block. At that same moment, Tish was calling Silence, crying her heart out telling him the same.

"What time did this shit happen?" Spizz asked the speaker on the other end of the phone. "So nobody saw shit, huh. All of y'all niggas out there and nobody saw shit?" Spizz was pissed as he yelled into the phone. "I'll handle this shit when I get back in town," he said before ending the call.

"I don't know, baby, but I'll find out," Silence said in an attempt to comfort his long-time girlfriend. "I will see you tonight though. In the meantime, keep ya mind right. Yeah, my love to you, too," Silence said before ending his call.

"The little nigga Haz said they rocked the lil bros and left everything in the crib," Spizz said to Silence, not able to believe what he just heard.

He had big plans for those two men. Both of them made him a lot of money since their dealings and now there was a gap in his organization, not to mention the loss he took as far as the money they owed him.

The part of town where they hustled made lucrative amounts of paper daily. With the war going on between their hoods, Spizz had no way into their drug market, until Dutch and Bullet came along.

"Guess it wasn't about the money then," Silence calmly said as he continued the drive to Philly.

It was normal for Silence to show no emotion, but how calm he was about the whole thing told Spizz he knew something. Silence has never been the type to share his plans or voice the reasons as to why he does anything, so Spizz was often left in the dark. Usually this never bothered him, but this time was different—he wanted answers.

Spizz sat in the passenger side silently for a minute, putting pieces together about what just happened to his lil homies. Shit didn't seem right, and not to mention Silence is behind the wheel driving as if nothing ever happened.

"Stop the fucking car, my nigga!" Spizz demanded.

Silence heard his friend but continued to drive for a few more miles before pulling into a Wawa gas station.

"That was ya work. That shit got Silence written all over it. What the fuck, brah? You leaving me in the dark now?" Spizz questioned Silence angrily about the whole situation.

Deep down he didn't really give a fuck that the little niggas were dead—well, that his man did it—he's cool. Spizz was more upset about not knowing what the fuck was going to happen and why. *I mean, he did have a lot of love for the young gunnas.*

Silence sat quiet for a few minutes before answering. "Are you done?"

Spizz just looked and nodded his head.

Silence hated to be questioned, even if it was by his right hand man. "Good! I do what needs to be done for us, and that's the end of it," Silence said before pulling out of the gas station to continue en route to Philly.

The rest of the way there they drove in silence, each deep in their own thoughts. Spizz knew that whatever went down, there was a good reason behind it, but his worries were not about the lives of these men; it was more so about his paper that Silence left behind.

"I saw the little nigga Dutch get bagged this morning. I sat down the block and watched." Silence finally spoke. "They pulled a choppa out of the truck, and from where I was sitting, it looked like a nice amount of work. Two hours later, I see the nigga at 7-11, as if everything was good. Now, what does that look like to you?" Silence asked.

Spizz sat there, taking in what Silence had just told him, knowing that what Silence did had to be done.

"Damn! If you would have never peeped that shit . . ."

"Right place, right time. I told you a long time ago and you should see it by now. Never question me . . . I do what needs to be done and that's how it will always be," Silence said as they pulled up to Reach's security gate.

"What the fuck. You could have at least grabbed the paper. That's what's really bothering me the most," Spizz shot back.

"Like I said, it wasn't about the money," Silence repeated.

The men left it at that and remained silent as they waited for Reach to buzz them in.

"This nigga living," Spizz said, amazed by the structure of Reach's mansion. "Rolls Royce, Bentley, and a Benz truck! This is what the fuck I'm talking about. This is how my shit gone be laid out," Spizz continued.

"Relax," Silence said, looking his friend dead in the eyes. "We here on business, nothing more."

Spizz has always been one to be fascinated by the finer things in life. Meanwhile, Silence does not really care for it. Modesty has always been his strong suit, and he knows how much his partner gets blinded by success. Right now, his head has to be in the game.

Reach greeted the two men at the door. He was a tall cat; at 6'5" and every bit of 260 pounds, he towered over both of them. Figure that is where he got his name.

Silence and Spizz were not small men by a long shot. Silence stood at 5'9" and weighed close to 240 pounds, all muscle, and Spizz stood at 5'10" and weighed 210 pounds. But, as it is known, the big shit means nothing.

"Y'all niggas want a drink?" asked Reach as he escorted them into his massive living room, which was decked out with marble floors, a big eighty-inch, flat-screen posted up on the wall, huge leather couches fit for a king, a grand piano in the corner, and a unlimited amount of artwork splattered all over the walls.

"Nah, no drinks. Let's just get down to why the fuck I am here!" Silence coldly said to Reach, unable to hide his hate for bitch niggas in position.

"I was just showing hospitality, trying to make sure you are comfortable in my home."

Reach spoke in a low voice, trying to ease the tension, while thinking to himself, *I knew this was a fucked up idea, especially letting these crazy-ass niggas know where the fuck I live.*

"What's the problem?" Spizz jumped in.

He gave his friend a look telling him to let him do the talking.

"Man, this nigga named Solo, from South Philly, keeps robbing all of my spots and sending word for me to pay him rent to keep shit going," Reach replied, puffing his chest out in a comical way as if he's certified of some sort. "This nigga been out of the game for the past five years, and now he is home gunning for all the money getters in the city," Reach continued, hoping that these two men could make this problem go away.

"Why couldn't any of ya own men handle it?" Spizz asked Reach, confused why their services were needed. This nigga had all this fucking money and niggas throughout the city moving his work yet call on them for a hit.

"Niggas said he's the Reaper, and if you don't wanna go to jail, then he is who you should call," Reach calmly answered, trying not to appear as nervous as he actually was.

"Tell me about this Solo nigga," Silence stepped in and asked, wondering how much he can get out of this fuck-ass nigga before he carried out his plan.

"The nigga ran South Philly for years before he went down on murder charges. He came home and basically took back what was his, and this trip he has this whole extortion scheme," Reach said to the men.

"So he's getting money, too?" asked Spizz, curious about his position in this whole ordeal.

"Yeah, boy, getting to a dollar. I mean, not like me, but he's in a nice position," Reach added, throwing his status out to thee to be heard.

"What's his life worth to you? And don't waste my fucking time," Silence warned.

"A hundred grand," was Reach's price on Solo's head.

"Well, my price is a quarter mil, nothing less. Take it or I'll leave you!" Silence said sternly, meaning every word.

Scared to death and not knowing what else to say, Reach agreed to what Silence had negotiated, well, demanded.

"Half up front. Half when it's done. Now go get our money," Silence ordered the man standing in front of them.

The money was all for Silence. Spizz got to keep all of the work and money he got from each spot. That's why he always wanted to ride with his brah.

It bugged the shit out of Spizz how Silence could just go to some nigga's crib, kill everybody there, and leave a couple hundred thousand or even millions behind; Spizz could never wrap his head around that shit.

Reach disappeared upstairs in his massive house while Silence and Spizz waited patiently for him to come back, money in hand.

"What you think, my nigga?" Spizz asked, breaking the silence.

"What do I think about what?" Silence responded without even looking at his friend.

Silence is in the zone, ready to murder and is not really beat for too much conversation, let alone answer anybody's questions.

Spizz, being Spizz, knew this but didn't really give a fuck. He just wanted to know what his brother was thinking about. Before he could push any further, Reach came back with a Gucci book bag filled with the $125,000 requested for this job. Well, half of what was requested.

"Now tell us everything you know about this nigga—where he lives, what he drives, hangouts, who he fucks with, and anything else that may be of use. Anything goes wrong because of what you told us, you die. Understood?" Silence questioned, getting into murder mode.

Over the next few hours, Reach covered every aspect of Solo's day-to-day actions, from where his baby mother lives, who stays with him, and how many niggas he keeps around him at all times.

"Boy is gonna definitely put up a fight. He ain't known to buckle and can stomach just about anything," Reach added.

"Give me a day or two," Silence told Reach before leaving his estate.

Silence is a very patient man, and he has been waiting for the nigga Reach's call for over six months now. Spizz thinks he's just another nigga to get paid off, but he'll soon realize that Reach is worth a little bit more than what Silence is making the situation out to be.

"I need some acid!" Silence told Spizz. He knew Spizz never agreed with his tactics, but Silence truly didn't care what he thought because it gets the job done and everybody leaves happy.

Spizz just shook his head at the request.

"So, when are we rolling out, my nigga?" Spizz asked, looking forward to the payday that was to come. But the question he asked himself was, *At what cost this time?*

"Tomorrow night, dress casual. And don't forget the acid; I'll bring the rope." Silence replied as he calculated each step that will be taken to get the job done, hoping that Reach was right about where Solo would be tomorrow night.

The rest of the ride back to the city was silent, with the exception of the music playing low in the backdrop. Each man was stuck in his own thoughts. At least for now.

CHAPTER

4

3 a.m. that night

"Baby, where have you been? I needed you and you wasn't here!" cried Tisha as Silence walked through the front door of their home in Sea Isle City.

She had been waiting for her man to come home. Silence was a smart man who followed the rules of the street. He knew his line of work and once he got his pockets where they needed to be, he moved most of his family out of the city. Him, Tish, and their daughter, Nazia, got a crib out of the way on a small island in the next county over.

"Things needed my attention, so I had to handle them," replied Silence as he kicked his shoes off before going over to comfort his wife-to-be.

"They killed him. They killed my brother. Why would someone do something like that?"

Tish was hysterical and Silence just held her. He knew how much it would hurt her if he killed her brother, but he had to protect himself as well as his right hand, Spizz.

"You knew he was in the streets, Tish, and that shit comes with it. I'm sorry about lil brah, but you sitting here crying and shit won't do nothing for Dutch. It damn sure won't bring him back!" Silence said, trying his best to comfort Tish in her time of need.

Silence was not really one to be emotional, and regretful about anything, but he does love Tish and hated seeing her like that.

"I want you to find out who did this shit, Silence, and I want you to kill them. Kill them for me. Make them suffer, Silence. Make them suffer!" Tish said as she went from emotional and hurt to rage.

Tish knew what Silence was into even though he has never talked to her about it, but the streets talk and she hears things. Her friends often ask her how could she be with a psycho like Silence, and her response every time was love.

Tish is a doctor at Shore Memorial Hospital, she's the one who puts the people to sleep for surgery, so you know she makes good money. That has always been her dream, and Silence helped her fulfill that dream by paying for her to go to school, which took a lot of money and a lot of time—seven years to be exact.

Who would think, a doctor fucking with a gangsta? That's the way that love works.

Tish's family live on the west side of the city and kept her away from niggas like Silence, but them sharing the same school led to where they were today.

"I'll handle it," Silence told his wifey, knowing that if he said he would take care of it, then it would be done.

Tish felt a lot better with the thought of Silence getting revenge for her only brother's death.

"Now let's go upstairs," Silence said very seductively as he pulled Tish towards their bedroom.

Tish was beautiful. At 5'1" and 125 pounds, she was petite but portioned out in the right places. She is a Redbone with dark brown hair, hazel eyes, and a smile that will melt any nigga's heart.

"Baby, I don't feel sexy right now. I'm hurt, and I have been crying all night and look a mess," Tish told Silence.

She knew he would make her feel much better than how she did at the moment and was looking forward for him to doing so.

"Come here," Silence said as he pulled Tish away from the bed towards the full-length mirror on her closet door.

"Do you know what I see when I look at you?" asked Silence as he removed her silk robe. Not giving her time to respond, he said, "I see perfection. And no matter where we are, what room we are in, and how many people are around . . . all that I am able to see is you. You are beautiful," he continued as he kissed her on her right shoulder blade.

Silence then turned Tish around and walked her back over to the bed, where he laid her down and kissed every inch of her body, making her feel like the queen she knew she was.

"Silence, I love you!" Tish moaned as he kissed her on her forehead.

Hearing this, Silence leaned back a little to take in the beauty of what laid beneath him, starting for a minute before speaking.

"My love goes to you as well, baby, and I wouldn't have it any other way," Silence said softly as he continued planting kisses all over her body.

"Baby, I want you to fuck me," Tish whispered to Silence.

She did not want to be made love to. She needed to get her mind fully off the incident with her brother earlier that day. And having her brain fucked out will do just that.

Those words were like music to his ears and hearing them turned him into a straight animal. He loved to fuck Tish because of how small she was. Silence grabbed both of her arms so she was unable to move as he put all nine inches of dick into her little frame.

Tish tried to say something, but before she could, Silence told her to shut the fuck up as he covered her mouth while holding both of her arms with one hand.

Silence thrusted away, hitting all of the spot that would drive any woman insane. Tish was loving every minute of it as her pussy dripped uncontrollably all over the sheets. Silence uncovered her mouth.

"You love this gangsta dick," he asked Tish between pumps.

"No!" Tish moaned with pure satisfaction, knowing her answer would do more justice than what was already being done.

"Good," Silence replied as he released Tish's hands.

He grabbed both of her legs and pushed them towards her shoulder. Tish tried to get away because this position drives her fucking crazy and she always loses control, but Silence was too strong and he violently pulled her back to the hard dick she so desperately just tried to get away from.

"Where are you going?" Silence asked Tish as he slammed his dick back into her gushing pussy.

Tish was unable to contain herself as she screamed and moaned while Silence gave her the fuck that she asked for.

"HMMM, HMMM . . ." Tish moaned as Silence started to long stroke.

Tish couldn't handle this, but she was unable to move because her legs were penned to his shoulder and Silence had both arms wrapped around them while holding both of her arms.

"OH SHITTTTT . . . WAIT . . . WAIT!" Tish screamed as she began to squirt, something she loved to do but could never handle.

Silence started to pound even harder, getting more excited as he saw Tish's cum dripping out of her pussy with each pump.

"You love this gangsta dick?" Silence questioned again, already knowing the answer that was about to come.

"A little bit," Tish moaned, knowing she loved him and his dick with all she has, but she knew this excited Silence even more.

Silence then released her hands and let her legs down. Tish took the opportunity to take flight, well, at least try. She pushed Silence with everything she had, knowing what was about to happen.

"Baby, wait. I gotta stop. I can't breathe!" Tish pleaded, knowing her pleas would fall on deaf ears. Secretly, this was what she really wanted.

"Shut the fuck up, and get back over here!" Silence replied, naked and out of breath, sweating like a madman.

"Baby, wait," Tish continued to plead as Silence walked over to where she was standing.

He picked her up as she tried to fight to get away, but was to weak.

Silence threw Tish back on the bed and turned her around on all fours before pile-driving back into Tish's swollen and dripping pussy. She loved every thrust.

"Relax," Silence told her as she continued to try to pull away.

Silence pounded and pounded, until both of their bodies collapsed after meeting their climax at the very same time.

"Do you love this gangsta dick yet?" Silence asked playfully as they both lay there, sweating and out of breath.

"Yes baby, I love both of you," Tish said before they fell asleep in each other's arms.

CHAPTER

5

The day of the hit

For Spizz, it was business as usual as he made his rounds throughout the city, dropping off work, picking up paper, and fucking random bitches.

"Bitch, get up. Ya time here is done," Spizz said to some chick named Tameeka that he occasionally fucked around with from time to time.

He had met up with her after dropping Silence of at his crib the night before.

"It is early as hell, Spizz. Damn, let me sleep," Tameeka slurred, still feeling the effects of their wild night.

Tameeka was the type of bitch that would cling to a nigga in hopes that it could be something more than what it was.

Don't get it twisted, though. Shorty was bad—a tall joint at 5'10", 155 pounds, built like Buffy, chocolate with gray eyes. Crazy, right? Pussy real good but shorty out there crazy, and Spizz wasn't about to tie down no ho, no bitch for that matter.

"I don't have time this morning, Meek. That's why I didn't really want to call ya ho ass, but I needed my dick sucked and I know you always down for the job," Spizz said in a very serious but comical type of way.

"Fuck you, Rahmir," Tameeka shot back, using Spizz's government.

"Yeah, I know. Now get the fuck out. I got shit to do today," Spizz replied, peeling off a stack for Tameeka for her services.

"I'm not a fucking ho, Rahmir, and I don't need ya money!" Tameeka shot back before getting dressed and walking out of the front door.

"Stupid bitch," Spizz mumbled to himself.

On the other side of town

"How much work we got left in the spot?" Aido asked Rico as he counted the rest of the money he planned on flipping with Spizz.

"Thirty-two bundles," Rico answered, annoyed as he served a fiend nigga out of the back window.

"Come on, youngin. I did what you asked and you promised to give me two. I come back every time," the old man tried to plead with Rico about the deal they made.

"Aight, old nigga, but if you not back by tonight, I'ma lock you in the fucking basement and watch you kick that shit. And you know how painful that is?" Rico joked with the old head.

"Aight, youngin, I'll be back," the old man said as he ran off, happy with what he had just received.

Aido and Rico have known each other for a few years now. Both were hungry savages that will get it by any means. They ran uptown as far as the dope game went and niggas haven't really challenged them because of their relationship with Silence and Spizz.

"Yo, my nigga. Did you ever get that info for Silence about the cat, B-Boy?" Aido asked his man, referring to this New York nigga that came through looking for their mentor.

"Nah, brah. Nobody have seen son since that day, and we don't have a pic of the dude to be passing around, so we gotta wait," Rico said.

He thought back to the day when he met B-Boy and wanted that trophy for his mentor, but Aido opted against it, wanting to know what Silence wanted to do.

"Spizz just pulled up," Aido said as he checked his phone after receiving a text from his big brah.

"Unlock the door, Rico. I don't want brah waiting," Aido continued as he put the rest of the paper in the bag for the work.

"What up, my goons?" Spizz asked his youngins as he walked into their spot.

Like Silence, Spizz had genuine love for these two young boys. About a year ago, some niggas puta bounty on Spizz's and Silence's heads, and who did they call? Aido and Rico, not knowing the ties these men had.

Long story short, Aido and Rico rocked the nigga and came back with his head in a bag, telling Silence and Spizz the science behind it. Ever since then, they knew where Rico and Aido were with their loyalty and it's been real since.

"Shit, my nigga. We waiting on you," Aido replied, wanting to get on with the deal because shit was about to start moving in just a few.

"Aight, cool. I gave you 150 walls. The prices dropped for me, so only for y'all it drops as well. Instead of the 150 a joint, the price is 100," Spizz continued, trying to move things along as well because he had to meet up with Silence to discuss the plans for their job tonight.

"That's love, big brah. And next trip being that prices are different, our flip is gone go up. You drop, we drop, so shit going move a lil faster, feel me?" Aido said, hoping to make his mentor proud.

"I expect nothing less. Where the fuck did Rico just go?" Spizz asked as he looked around, confused 'cause he was hoping to have a word his other youngin.

"He 'bout to go take care of something that's standing in our way. He never tells me shit, so I be blind to what the fuck be going on. All I know is that he leaves, next thing you know a nigga is dead."

"I know exactly what you deal with," Spizz shot back as he walked out of the door, smiling while thinking about how Silence has the same tactics.

3 p.m. that same day

"Baby, I gotta go," Silence told Tish as he got dressed after they showering together.

"I was hoping to spend some time with you today, Silence. You know . . . the kind of thing that real couples do," Tish responded in a very sarcastic way.

"Not today," Silence replied very casually as he picked his phone up to text Spizz and tell him to meet him in the hood.

"When will you be back?" Tish asked with the saddest look on her face. She knew when Silence disappears, it was not just for a few hours, but a few days.

Tish didn't worry about other females. Her only concern was Silence making it home by any means, hoping he could avoid jail and play smart enough to avoid getting killed.

"Can't say, so be patient," Silence said, kissing Tish on the forehead before walking out of the door.

Back around the hood, Spizz sat on the wall watching the project traffic. Who would have thought he would control the dope game in and around the hood? All thanks to Silence though.

When Spizz first got started in the drug game quietly, Silence started to murder anybody who stood in Spizz's way. In his mind, if you weren't getting it from his man, then you die and get it from no one.

Silence had never sold drugs nor profited from Spizz's operation. They had a mutual understanding—that your hustle belonged to you and mine to me; and it worked out perfectly.

"Yo, big brah. Shit been hot since Bino rocked that nigga top around the corner. You know information don't really come out the hood, so these pigs be patrolling extra crazy son!" said Rican, Spizz's hood captain.

"Numbers are still good though, so I ain't tripping off that," Spizz told his youngin.

Rican was a boss in his own right and a lot of little niggas looked up to son, plus he was known for putting niggas to rest. On top of that, he kept the projects in line when Spizz and Silence couldn't be around.

"I'ma get with you some other time, lil brah. Me and Silence gotta talk about something," he said, finishing up the conversation with Rican as Silence pulled up in the Range.

"Aight, my nigga. Be safe," Rican said as he went over to Silence's truck to greet his other man. "Si, what up?" Rican asked in passing.

"Life," was Silence's only and typical response.

"What up, my goon?" Spizz said as he hopped in the passenger side of Silence's wheels.

"Business," replied Silence, wanting to run down the details while avoiding everything else that might come up in conversation.

Spizz was the type of nigga that got sidetracked quickly and Silence hated that about his friend, especially when it came to the severity behind the line of work Silence was involved in.

"Aight, so what's the plan?"

"You're going to play the club. Reach said Solo goes to Onyx every Saturday night, so you will be there to be sure he goes straight home afterwards."

"How the fuck am I supposed to do that? What, you want me to kidnap the nigga?" Spizz shot back.

Silence ignored his friend as he sat quiet for a minute, trying not to spazz on his brother for cutting him off. Spizz has a habit of doing that and if he had been anybody else, he'd be dead.

"Before you cut me off, let me finish," Silence sternly said to Spizz. "As I was saying, you will assure that he goes straight home. He'll be there with one of his cannons, but that won't be an issue. All you gotta do is slip him this," Silence said, passing Spizz two Roxy 30s. Mixed with liquor, it would put anybody down for the count.

"Once he's all passed out in the club, the nigga he's with will have no other choice than to get him home—and that's where I will be waiting. While you are with him, I will go to his house and handle things there. In and out," Silence finished.

"Aight, but what is the acid for?" Spizz asked, confused about what Silence could want it for.

"I don't need it . . . You do," Silence said to Spizz. "Reach said he doesn't break easy, and you do want what he has, am I correct?" Silence asked, knowing that at the end, he would be the one using it.

"So we torturing this nigga?" Spizz asked, already knowing the answer.

"I'm there for his life; you're there for what he has, so yes," Silence said as he pulled off after letting Spizz out.

"This nigga crazy," Spizz said to himself as he got into his cream-colored 7601i.

Spizz knew that this was going to be a long night. He was well-prepared for it. Spizz loved being there for his nigga, plus he knew that Silence would not be the only one getting paid tonight. And in the back of his mind he wanted to get to know the cat Reach a little better. Seeing how he lived and all, maybe he can be of some benefit to both him and Silence. He will soon find out.

CHAPTER

6

Later that night

Solo and his second-in-command were just arriving at the night club they frequently visited to wind down and ease the stress from the streets. As always, the club was jumping, with lines stretched around the corner. This was no problem for Solo, being that he was one of the top niggas in Philly, and not to mention a certified killer.

"Leek, what up, my boy?" Solo greeted one of the bouncers at the entrance of the club as he handed him a few hundreds to get his strap past security. He knew that a lot dudes wanted him dead and would love to catch him slipping without it.

"Same shit, trying to keep most of these fuck-ass jokers out of the door; half of these cats are only here to try and catch a lick. You know how that goes!" Leek replied as he let Solo and his shooter into the packed night club.

Spizz has been there for about an hour now, waiting for Solo to come through. He sat at the bar, chopping it down with one of the strippers he knew from down the way.

Spizz was no stranger to spots like this. Looking at him, you could tell that his money was type long.

Dressed in Armani from head to toe, with a custom Rolex icier than the streets of Alaska, and more money in his pockets than the average corner boy had in his stash, no one would ever think that he was here to lure a man to his death.

"Lee Lee, I need you to do something for me. I promise it will be worth ya while," Spizz said in shorty's ear over the loud music blasting from the club's speakers.

Lee Lee was one of them bitches that be in the club setting out-of-town niggas up to get robbed. Shorty has always been a grimy bitch, but looking at her, you can never tell. Fuck a ten, this bitch is a twelve, so you can only imagine how many sucka's came in trying to take her home, some even looking to wife her. Lee was down for whatever though, as long as she got her paper.

"Anything for you, Spizz," Lee Lee replied while kissing him on his cheek.

"See that cat over there with that big-ass chain on?" Spizz said, pointing her in the direction of Solo at the other end of the bar buying drinks for everybody around him.

"Who, Solo?" Lee Lee asked, already knowing who he was, him being a regular there and all.

"Yeah, you know him?" Spizz answered, noticing that Lee Lee was already familiar with his target. In his mind, that was a good thing.

"Yes. He spends big money and loves my company," Lee Lee said, smiling, knowing that this favor that Spizz is about to ask will have her leaving the club loaded tonight.

"I'll give you five racks to drop this in his drink, and I will take it from there," Spizz said as he gave Lee Lee the crushed up pills Silence gave him earlier that night.

"Done!" was all Lee Lee said before making her way over to where Solo and a few niggas were sitting.

Meanwhile, at Solo's spot . . .

Silence had been sitting in the dark in Solo's kitchen table for quite a few hours now, waiting for Solo's wife and daughter to come home.

In the back of his mind, he hoped the child stayed with someone else instead of coming home with her mother for tonight. He didn't like killing children, but a witness is a witness and no one gets left alive— that is a rule that never gets broken.

Unlike Spizz, Silence is very patient. You have to be in his line of work, so waiting there does not bother him, he just hoped Spizz played his part and didn't fuck up.

On the table were three ropes and a container of acid that he had Spizz get from one of his many resources. Silence loved to torture niggas. He got a thrill from seeing them suffer, and never had remorse from taking someone's life. That is why, over time, niggas started referring to him as the Reaper. No bounty was ever turned down.

"I could have sworn I left the lights on," Stephanie said as she walked through the door, bags in hand.

Stephanie was Solo's wife. She rode with him for the ten he did upstate. They had a fourteen-year-old daughter together and a baby on the way.

Relieved that their daughter did not walk through the door with her mother, Silence continued waiting for the right moment to appear out of the darkness.

Stephanie walked toward the kitchen with the bags she struggled to carry into the house. When she hit the light switch in the kitchen, she noticed Silence sitting there with a gun pointed at her.

"Don't scream, don't move, and don't be stupid," Silence told Stephanie as he sat at the head of the table eating a bowl of cereal as if he belonged there. "Come . . . have a seat," he said between bites. as he guided her where to sit using his gun.

"What do you want?" Stephanie asked as she shook uncontrollably. "I am pregnant. Please don't hurt me. We have money, if that is what you came for. I don't know where it is, but we have it!" she pleaded.

Silence sat there and stared at the woman as if she was already dead. He felt no emotion. To him, this was just a job and it's unfortunate that this woman was pregnant, but fuck it.

"Relax," was all Silence said to Stephanie as he started to tie her to the chair.

Back at the club

"Lee Lee, what's up, baby girl? You leaving with me tonight or what?" a drunk Solo asked Lee Lee as she sat on his lap.

"I'll go anywhere you want me to," Lee Lee said as she kissed Solo, distracting him from his drink that he just ordered.

With quickness and experience, she slipped the powdery substance in his drink without anyone noticing. They were in a strip club, so nobody was really paying attention anyway.

Spizz sat across from the bar, watching Lee Lee do her thing while he thought to himself how Silence was going to kill her, too. *No loose ends*, Silence always stressed.

"Let me get you a drink," Solo slurred as he downed the shot sitting in front of him.

"Maybe later, baby. I'm next on stage," Lee Lee said as she kissed him on the cheek and headed to the back of the club to change. Passing Spizz on her way to the dressing room, Lee Lee mouthed to him, "I'll call you when I leave tonight."

In her mind, she *just made the easiest five thousand in her life and didn't even have to fuck for it*, she thought to herself.

Spizz sat there, babysitting his drink and waiting for the pills to kick in on Solo, which didn't take very long. A few minutes later, Solo could be seen nodding in and out in his VIP booth across the room.

Now all that was left was for his men to see this and get him home.

About a half hour later, you could see two men carrying Solo out of the club. From where Spizz was sitting, Solo looked passed out all the way. He hoped Silence's plan worked and they would take him home instead of somewhere else. He headed toward the exit, so he could follow whatever car the men were getting into.

As Spizz followed their car, he noticed they were indeed heading for Solo's crib. Spizz began to wonder if the men will stick around or put him on his couch and go on their own way. No matter the case, Spizz was just happy that everything was going right for the moment.

As they pulled up to the house, it looked as if nobody was home. Stephanie's car could not be seen because she had parked it in the garage.

Silence heard the front door unlock and raised his gun at the kitchen entrance in case one of Solo's men decided to come in and get comfortable. He had no problem killing extra men, so being nervous was far from what he felt at that moment.

Outside, Spizz was parked across the street, watching the men carry Solo into the house. He then saw a light come on and, a few seconds later, both men exited the house, hopped back in their car, and pulled off.

Relieved that the men didn't stick around, Spizz got out of his car. He went to knock on the front door, but Silence had the door already open as Spizz was walking up the driveway.

"You ready?" Silence asked Spizz as they proceeded to tie Solo to the chair next to his wife.

"Let's do this," Spizz replied.

After tying Solo up and gagging him, Silence pulled out a packet of amonia. As Solo came to, he was a little thrown off at first because he couldn't move. Once he realized what was going on, he began to rock back and forth violently trying to get loose.

"Relax," Silence said very calmly while sitting back at the head of the table. Both Solo and Stephanie sat on both sides of him. At this point, Stephanie, as you can realize, was a mess, not knowing what was going to happen and still hoping these men would not harm her and her unborn child.

Spizz stood behind Solo with his gun pointed at the back of his head. Silence reached over to pull the gag from his mouth, so he could speak.

"This won't take long," Silence said to Solo as he lit his blunt that he had behind his ear.

"Do y'all niggas know who the fuck I am?" shouted Solo. Like that would even matter at this point.

"You're a man that is about to die," Silence responded in between hitting his blunt that he had been smoking prior to Solo's arrival.

"Where is the money?" Spizz cut in, asking Solo.

"That's what this is about? Y'all niggas are here to rob me?" Solo asked, still not able to believe niggas had enough heart to try something like this.

"I'm here for your life," Silence scolded him, correcting the man about a robbery.

"Whoever sent you, I will double it," Solo said confidently in hopes that these men would take the bait.

"No deal. I honor all contracts, and you are next," Silence told Solo, letting him know nothing could change the outcome of his fate.

Sensing that Solo was going to make the situation more difficult than it needed to be, Silence got up and walked behind Stephanie. He pulled out a glass medicine bottle filled with acid. He pulled the cap off and started to fill up the dropper with the deadly liquid.

"Tick . . . tock!" Silence said as he pulled Stephanie's chair from under the table, exposing her pregnant belly.

Solo sat there stone-faced, not saying a word.

'Tick . . . tock!" Silence repeated, lifting Stephanie's shirt over her baby bump.

Stephanie began to go crazy, rocking from side to side in the chair, as if this would stop what was about to happen.

Silence then squeezed a single drop onto Stephanie's exposed belly and watched her scream in agony.

"Where is the money?" Spizz asked again, getting frustrated with the whole situation.

Solo continued to sit there, not saying anything.

"So you're gonna just sit and watch your unborn child die?" Spizz questioned again as Silence continued to squeeze drop after drop, going back and forth from Stephanie's belly to the top of her head.

At this point, Stephanie had lost consciousness and just sat there, head hanging low, as the smell of burned flesh filled the room.

"Tick . . . tock," Silence said as he was about to squeeze a few more drops onto to Stephanie's pregnant belly.

Coming to his senses, Solo gave up and told Spizz everything he wanted to know.

"Kill me, but just let her live man. She has nothing to do with this—"

Before Solo could continue, Silence shot Stephanie twice in the head and once in the stomach.

Solo couldn't believe what he just saw. He was unable to move or say anything.

Meanwhile, Spizz went and retrieved the money that Solo said was upstairs. Silence sat back down, watching Solo frozen in his chair.

"We good, my nigga," Spizz said as he reentered the kitchen carrying a duffel bag over his right shoulder.

Silence then stood and shot Solo three times in the head before he and Spizz headed towards the door.

"Time to collect," Silence said as they got into Spizz's car that was parked across the street.

CHAPTER

7

Reach's estate

"That shit should be taken care of real soon. I put some real right niggas on the job," Reach said into receiver of his cell phone.

"If shit go how I expect it to, then I'ma put these two jokers on my payroll," Reach continued.

Reach didn't have too many people that he trusted and tended to stay real low and off the radar. That's why it was so hard for outsiders to even get to him.

He was never meant to be in position, but took over things when his older brother went to the feds a few years back. Niggas in the streets didn't really respect him, but he treated niggas fairly—mostly out of fear, though.

"Yo, I'ma hit you back, my nigga. I gotta check up on the wife and the kids. They out Delaware visiting her family. Yeah, no doubt. I'll keep you posted," Reach said before hanging up to call and check on his family.

Before he could call his wife, the intercom to the front gate went off.

"Who the fuck could this be?" Reach asked himself, not expecting anybody over for tonight. He went into his security room to check the cameras and saw Silence and Spizz in the car outside the gate.

He buzzes them in, wondering why they didn't call before they came.

"What up, boy?" Reach said, greeting the men at his front door. "I wasn't expecting y'all niggas this late. I thought maybe y'all would call

39

before coming," Reach said, really wanting to know why they didn't do so.

"Phone died!" Silence said in a low pitch before closing the door behind them.

"So, is it done?" Reach asked, figuring that was what the men were doing back at his home, and especially at this time of night.

"I wouldn't be here if it wasn't," Silence said with a menacing smile on his face, appearing a lot friendlier than their last meeting.

Spizz noticed this too, but brushed it off as nothing. I mean, when it's all said and done, business is business.

"Cool, I'll go get the rest of your money," Reach said as he disappeared upstairs to pay out what is owed.

"Yo, what's up with you? Why are you being so friendly with son?" Spizz questioned, knowing his friend far too well.

Silence ignored Spizz as he scanned the room, noticing the many cameras placed throughout the house. As Spizz began to speak again, Reach appeared with another bag filled with the other half of the money that was agreed upon.

"You want to count it?" Reached asked Silence as he handed the bag to him.

"Nah, but you can take me to your security room, where you keep all of the recording," Silence said as he aimed his gun at Reach's head.

Caught off guard but aware of what was going on, Reach began to stutter as he dropped to his knees and pleaded for his life.

"I paid you what you wanted. What the fuck is going on?" Reach asked, realizing it was a big mistake having these men meet him at his home. He did not know it wouldn't have made a difference where they met—he still had to die.

Spizz just stood there, just as confused as Reach. He knew Silence wasn't the robbing type, so what the fuck was going on?

Not wanting to question his brother at the moment, he went along with it.

"Take us to the security room," Spizz said as he pulled out his gun and aimed at Reach's head.

"I got more money upstairs. Y'all can have it. Just take it and go. Y'all will never hear from me again . . . Please, just let me be. I got a family," Reach begged, still on his knees but this time crying.

Silence was disgusted by this grown-ass man crying and begging for them to let him live.

"It's not about the money. I'm here for your life. I've been waiting for your call for quite some time, and now here we are," Silence replied in a calm demeanor.

Spizz and Reach were more confused than ever, but Spizz just held his ground. He'll get to the bottom of this some other time.

"I've never seen you before in my life. I just got yah number from my man out ya way that be flipping work with me," Reach said, trying to plead for his life again.

"Security room," Silence repeated before lifting Reach to his feet.

The men proceeded down a long foyer before reaching the security room. Once inside, Silence disconnected the server and took out the hard drive that held the security footage from all cameras in and around the house.

He then pulled a box cutter from his back pocket and went over to slice Reach's throat. Before he got to do so, Spizz asked Reach where the money was. Silence stopped him, letting him know they were not there for the money. This time, it was personal.

"Who sent you?" Reach asked before his neck was slit from ear to ear.

"God!" Silence responded as Reach's body fell to the floor.

After grabbing the security footage from the computers, they exited the room and headed for the front door to leave Reach's estate with the money Reach had just paid Silence.

As they got into the car to drive away, Silence dialed a number and waited a few seconds for someone to answer.

"It's done," was all he said into his phone as they drove back to Atlantic City from Philadelphia.

Most of the ride back was silent. Spizz was still kind of lost as to what just happened, and was even more pissed at the fact that they left all of that money in Reach's crib.

"Yo, my nigga, are you going to tell me what the fuck is going on or what?" Spizz asked his best friend as they drove.

Silence, as always, didn't answer right away. Instead, he just cut the music up a little more, letting Spizz know now was not the time.

As they hit the A.C. Expressway, Silence finally spoke. "There was a tag on his head. I waited eight months to get the nigga. Son was so scary, it was like he didn't exist, so I sat patiently up until the moment he reached out to me," Silence continued.

He paid the toll and proceeded on their way.

"Why the fuck didn't you tell me what was going on, kid?" Spizz questioned, still mad about the money.

"When do I ever?" Silence shot back, hating being questioned by his right hand man.

"Aight, cool. I respect that, but what made this time so different? I mean we left all that fucking paper in the crib!" Spizz said, mad as fuck that he couldn't get to the big money he knew was there.

About a year ago, Reach was dealing with some niggas out of D.C. pm the dope tip. He wasn't fucking with them very long, but he gained their trust, especially since each trip was a half mil in them D.C. nigga's pockets.

A few months into their business, Reach did some nut shit and ten kilos of heroin got seized upon leaving Philly. Word is that Reach started fucking with this new connect down in Miami without telling the D.C. niggas. They had an agreement that a shipment would arrive in Philly every Friday until both parties say otherwise. When the last shipment came through, them D.C. niggas called and called to ask Reach where the fuck he was at, but the nigga never answered. Growing tired of waiting they said "fuck it" and headed back to D.C. On their way leaving the city, they were flagged and got popped with the ten kilos.

Niggas tried hitting Reach to ask him what the fuck happened. They were gonna make him pay that half mil for that work since it was his fault that shit went back, but the nigga went under the radar. That's when them D.C. niggas got in touch with Silence.

"Like I said, this time, it was personal. Son pretty much burned one of his plugs, and all they wanted was his life."

42

"I asked if they wanted the paper he owed, and it was clear that his life was payment enough,", Silence said. "That's what I agreed to, so that is what it was," he continued.

"We still could have got that paper, my nigga. I mean, the nigga had millions," Spizz replied, not letting this shit go.

Silence sat there for a moment thinking about what his friend was saying. It made sense, but his code of conduct was more important.

"Sometimes you have to sacrifice, especially when it came to your word and reputation. Yeah, the money was free and it made sense for us to take it, but this was a hit, and it should be made to look like one. Don't be among those that has greed as a weakness. That shit is a disease that devours men, and you should be able to control that." Silence asked his friend, "You know how much money I could have if I were greedy? A lot. But I am content with what I am paid for. Why else do you think I have never once asked about how much you got from one of my victims? Once the contract is put in place, my only job is to take life," Silence continued as they pulled into their city. "I take souls for a living, and I honor my word while doing so. And that is why the money is still where it belongs."

Spizz sat there thinking about what Silence had just said. After it was broken down, it made more sense to him and he respected how his brother handled business. But he still thought he's crazy for leaving all of that paper behind.

CHAPTER

8

"Clear the block," Rican yelled out as the hood began to flood with police.

This was nothing unusual. In fact, it was pretty typical for the hood Silence and Spizz called home to be raided. These projects stretch across a three-block radius and is home to the city's grimmest goons, but the love and respect they had for each other was truly genuine.

"This is the third time this week," Rozay said to Rican as they hit one of the main trap houses.

Rican knew they would be coming, so they had time to get all of the work out of the crib before the pigs came through. Some cat he went to school with worked in the narcotics department in the city; he owed Rican big time for saving his life and his career a few years back, so as payment, he would inform Rican of any raids and informants that may be involved.

Although he didn't have to, Rican generously compensated his inside source for his services.

"Yeah, shit hot, and then papi niggas is making the situation even worse," Rican replied.

He was referring to the shooting that took place a few days ago, when them niggas came through trying to kill anyone who was on the block in hopes of avenging the murder of one of their own.

"What you want me to do about that situation, my nigga?" Rozay asked Rican. "I'm tired of these fuck-ass niggas," he continued.

Rozay was one of the young boys from the hood that loved to put in work; shoot-first-ask-questions-last kinda nigga and his hustle game was mean, but his temper overrode that sometimes. Especially when it came to the Dominican cartel; with them, it's personal for Rozay.

Word is that a couple of them niggas robbed, tied up, and killed his right-hand man, Swag, while he was doing time in juvenile detention. So, any green light he can get on them goya beans, he'd gladly take it.

"For now, we wait. We gotta be smart. Fuck taking out the little shooters. I want the boss. I got Fresh from A.V., on the mission as we speak now. He just started fucking the nigga Paco's baby mom, so we gone see where he gets with that," Rican replied.

Paco ran the south side in the next town over; niggas called it the boarder. Quite a few of them run shit and all of them are hard to get to because their money was super long. These niggas had car lots and all types of crazy shit, but Paco was the one that was wanted the most because he was the one who controlled the shooters.

"You ever tell Silence and Spizz about these niggas?" Rozay questioned, curious as to why they hadn't gotten involved by now.

"Nah, this is my problem. They gave the hood to us, so we gone hold it up the way they are expecting us to. But if things do happen to get to out of hand, I'ma holla at them niggas. But for now, we gotta find somewhere to move all this fucking work, 'cause these pigs are really starting to slow money up," Rican said, wanting to get rid of the 1,500 bricks that Spizz dropped off the day before.

"Fresh said he got a spot out Sicklerville that we can lay up in. Some nigga he was locked up with is from out there and said shit sweet and dope is garbage, so if the work is fire, then the streets will be ours," Rican continued.

Spizz cruised up the block, annoyed as he looked around and saw all of the squad cars and police surrounding the projects. He knew this was bad for business. He just hoped that his little homies could manage to compromise and move that work by any means necessary . . . because time is money, with no rewind and every second counts.

"Get in," Spizz said to Rican and Rozay as he pulled up behind one of the squad cars blocking the street.

He pulled away from the block and asked Rican about this cat named B-Boy that has been looking for Silence to see if maybe they heard something about him from somewhere.

"Ain't nobody come through looking for brah, especially not in the hood, 'cause nine times out of ten he wouldn't have made it out. But who is the nigga?" Rozay questioned, wondering who the fuck would be asking about Silence.

"Nobody knows. Aido said one of his young boys told him this New York nigga came through driving some big shit asking about Silence," Spizz said as he parked on the next block over.

He did not like that some nigga was out there looking for his brother; even worse, that they couldn't even put a face to the name.

"I'ma look into this nigga, but if I find him, do you want him dead?" Rican asked, ready to ride for his niggas.

"Nah. At least, not yet. Silence wants to meet son," Spizz said before switching to a more serious question. "Can y'all handle this shit or what?" Spizz asked, referring to what had been going on in the hood—the shooting and all of the raids.

"Yeah, we got it, my nigga. But rushing will cause confusion, casualties, and more heat. We gone start at the top and kill our way down, but we wanna keep it out of the city, 'cause all that shit is doing is slowing up work. Fiends scared to come through, thinking they gone get shot and shit. But we got a spot O.T. that we gone flood until this shit dies down, so the money will still be right," Rican said as he lit his blunt.

"That's what I expected to hear. Now let's get the fuck outta here. I have plans for us tonight," Spizz said as he pulled off.

He and Silence love spending time with their youngins, so every so often he took them out to get them away from the madness for a minute. Sometimes, they needed that.

That evening . . .

"Oh, shit. You scared the shit out of me. Don't be creeping up on me like that!" Lee Lee said playfully after catching Silence walking up behind her as she put the key in her front door to get in.

Lee Lee lived downtown over by the casinos. She, Silence, and Spizz all went to school together. Silence used to fuck with her back in the day . . . before she started hoeing and setting niggas up. They remained cool over the years, but Silence kept his distance for many reasons, one being that he still had a lot of love for her, and you can't love a grimy bitch.

Silence said nothing to her. He just stared through dark eyes for a second before pulling his gun.

"What are you doing, Si," Lee Lee asked as she began to get nervous, knowing his history and how he conducted his business.

"SHHHH," was all Silence said before shooting Lee Lee three times in the face and then walking off.

Walking back to his car, he felt no remorse for what he had just done. Even though he still had love for her, he believed her life was a means for him to continue to live freely . . . "No loose ends" was his number one rule.

Just a few blocks over, at the same time

"Excuse me, pretty girl," B-Boy said.

He stood in front of a bodega a few blocks from Bally's casino, trying to talk to one of the passing prostitutes.

"You pimping?" the prostitute asked very defensively, not wanting to be seen talking to another pimp.

"Nah, baby. I just need to know where I can find a nigga named Silence, that's all," B-Boy said with his hands raised, sensing how nervous she was.

The prostitute studied him over for a second before answering. "You shouldn't be out here asking for him, and I can tell you're not from around here because if you were, then you'd know where to look and most certainly wouldn't be out here asking about that crazy-ass nigga," the prostitute said.

She began to walk off, not wanting anything to do with him or that conversation.

"Damn, motherfuckers out here are that scared of this nigga?" B-Boy thought to himself as he walked back to his car.

B-Boy was from Harlem, and he had been back and forth to A.C. quite a few times in hopes of bumping into to Silence. He was a heavy particular thing that caused him to seek outside help; he was beginning to weigh in on him and he knew he couldn't handle it himself nor can he put his team on it.

Silence's name floated all over. Niggas say son is smart as hell, never leaving behind a trace of evidence and has no limit when it comes to murder.

"The Reaper" is what they called him, and when B-Boy heard of this, he knew that Silence would be right for the job. He could have easily tried calling or having somebody else do so, but B-Boy doesn't trust technology. And in his mind, everything is wired and phones can't be trusted, especially when it came to homicide. That way, nothing can tie him to Silence just in case the situation doesn't go right.

—ɱ—

"Pack a bag, we're going to Boston," Silence said into the receiver, with Spizz on the other end of the phone. "I'll meet you at ya crib," he continued before hanging up while thinking about the phone call he got prior to calling his friend.

—ɱ—

"Is this Silence?" a woman asked into the phone as soon as he picked up.

"Who are you?" Silence responded, curious as to who and why this woman was calling him.

"This is Princess. I'm calling about Julio," the woman replied as Silence sat on the other end of the line, not responding but thinking for a second.

"And?" he finally answered, still a bit curious.

"Can you be in Boston within the next twenty-four hours?" the woman questioned, hoping Silence would agree.

"Text an address," he said before hanging up.

Silence knew exactly who Julio was. He had done quite a few jobs for him over the years. In fact, Julio could have taken the easy way out by giving up Silence; he could have got a much lighter sentence had he cooperated about the murders.

Julio was charged with all types of kingpin charges, conspiracy, and about eight murders that were committed through Silence's hands. But him being the boss that he was, he stood his ground and wore his shit like a man without bringing niggas down with him.

Silence had a lot of respect for Julio, and would do just about anything for him. He has met Princess a few times, but it never went as far as a head nod. For her to be calling, and not Julio, was kind of strange—even for him—especially since Julio was doing life in the Feds out in Colorado. Whatever the case maybe, Silence will soon find out.

CHAPTER
9

"You wanna tell me what we're doing out here, my nigga?" Spizz asked Silence as their plane landed in Boston.

"I don't know yet. A car should be here to pick us up and take us where we need to be. I got a call asking if I could be here within twenty-four hours. And now that we are here, we will find out why together," Silence replied.

Outside of the airport waited an older White guy holding a sign that read, "Princess waits."

Silence didn't want his or Spizz's name used, so he decided to have her use hers as a means for him to know which car was there to pick them up.

He still didn't know if he could trust the situation, but he owed it to Julio to find out; for all he knew, this could be some kind of trap.

The ride to meet with Princess was longer than what Silence remembered, but he didn't mind at all; he loved having extra time to think when he was out on a mission, especially one where he didn't know what to expect.

"What you thinking about, kid?" Spizz asked his childhood friend, just as curious as he was about the whole trip.

"Life," Silence responded, not really wanting to get into conversation at this moment.

It bothered Spizz that Silence was so quiet and didn't talk much, but he's used to it, as Silence had been like this his whole life. But, at times like these, Spizz wished his brother wasn't a mute. He never knew what Silence was actually thinking, let alone what he was up to. What he did know was that Silence was smart, and that he thought about every detail before they did a job, so getting caught was the furthest thing from his mind.

As they arrived at Silence's old friend's home, they were greeted by one of the most beautiful women either of them had ever seen.

She was 5'9", had long brown hair and perfect bronze complexion, was petite, and had a thick Brazilian accent. "Princess" fit her just right.

"Thank you. My husband will be glad you could make it." Princess said as she shook both of their hands. "Come on in. Make yourselves comfortable while I go get the letter my husband instructed me to give to you," she continued as she escorted them into the living area.

"Damn, my nigga. I want her," Spizz said to Silence as Princess left to retrieve the letter sent for Silence.

"This is business!" Silence sternly replied, knowing how his brother was when it came to beautiful women. Before Spizz was able to respond, Princess walked in with a folded piece of paper and handed it to Silence.

"His lawyer brought this to me yesterday. I haven't opened it. I was instructed to call you and give it to you if you decided to come," Princess said as she watched Silence open the letter and begin to read.

My Friend,

If you are reading this, I want to thank you for coming; it really means a lot. I know that you are wondering why I sent for you, so I will get straight to the point.

My brother Marco has become a bit of a stranger over these past few months. When I went away, we had an agreement that every two weeks he would give my wife $250,000. Everything has been fine up until now. First I thought, well maybe the guy is locked up or something, but then that went out of the window because you know in here, you hear things.

People say he feels the need not to pay me anymore, saying that I am never coming home and that the business is his now. Do you know how that makes me feel? My own brother, someone who I gave the world to; without me, he would have been nothing. And this is how he repays me.

I know this may seem harsh, but I want him dead. Family or no family, disloyalty results in death, and at this point he is no different than others I have had killed. So I will give you $500,000 in exchange for taking his life; but you must cut off his hands for payments not due and before you kill him, make sure he is aware of who sent you.

I must warn you that he's extremely hard to get close to, so this may or may not require a lot of time, but you are the professional, so I have no doubt it will be done at the best time possible.

Before you leave my home, my wife will give you all of the money up front, only if you are willing to accept this job. Fly safe, my friend, and remember that loyalty is more than just a word; it is a way of life.

Your Friend

After reading the letter, Silence sat there for a few minutes thinking about what he had just read. He had no intention of turning this job down, especially for an old friend he owed so much to.

"Do you have a lighter?" Silence asked Princess as he folded the letter and placed it back in the envelope in which it came.

"Yes, give me a second," Princess responded as she disappeared into the kitchen.

"So, what's the plan?" Spizz asked, seeing the seriousness of Silence's face.

Whatever the case, Spizz was down to ride—not just because of a payday, but for his brother as well. Spizz knew that Silence was extremely smart and can handle any situation by himself, but a piece of him didn't like leaving Silence alone when it came to situation like this because things could always go wrong and you never knew what to expect.

"You are about to come into a lot of money," Silence said while looking dead into Spizz's eyes.

Princess returned with a box of wooden matches that she to Silence. She watched him walk over to the fireplace to set the letter on fire. They watched it burn to ash.

"Do you agree?" Princess asked.

She was instructed to pose this question as soon as Silence finished the letter. She knew not to give him the money unless he agreed to what her husband asked.

Normally, Silence would not do business with a woman of Princess's nature, but he knew her background. When Julio was first arrested, she was also detained and questioned, and to every one's surprise, she did not give the police any information. Most niggas in her shoes would talk with no hesitation, but the love she had for her man restrained her from doing so, so Silence saw no reason to not trust her wholeheartedly.

"Indeed," was Silence only response.

Princess then went into a hallway closet and dragged a big black duffel bag out, sliding it in front of Silence. She then dug into the side pocket and handed Silence the keys to a black Charger that was parked outside.

Inside the bag were several hand guns with silencers, along with the $500,000 that Julio promised for the job. After saying goodbye and loading the car with the bag of money and guns, Silence and Spizz got into the car and pulled away from Julio's home.

"He wants me to kill his brother," Silence told Spizz as they drove through Boston looking for a hotel they can stay at until the job was done.

"His brother?" Spizz, replied wanting to make sure he was hearing correctly.

"Yes!"

As they drove, Silence broke down the whole story to Spizz—about Julio and his brother Marco. He explained that when Julio was home, Marco was nothing more than a money counter; and when Julio went away, he gave Marco everything, and now he didn't want to continue paying.

Silence further explained that Julio was the one he would come and see when he told Spizz that he was up top. He further explained all of the murders and how Julio got arrested and spared Silence's life.

"Damn, I feel the nigga, but a hit on his brother though," Spizz again asked, still not able to digest the situation.

"The streets are the streets," Silence said as they pulled into the Marriot Hotel.

After checking into a room, Silence went over the plan with Spizz as to how they will get to Marco. Julio's letter to Silence included Marco's address, along with Marco's wife's schedule.

"He keeps two bodyguards with him at all times, and all of his cars are armored. Julio said the nigga was a straight bitch and is scary as all hell, so I see no problem for you to get what you want. All we have to do is get to this cat," Silence explained.

"He has a major a security system, so first we have to work on getting past that. He also has a few Great Danes around the property, but they won't be a problem. Catching his guards off guard will be the issue," Silence continued.

Spizz listened intently as his brother spoke. He didn't like the idea of killing your own brother, but fuck it, niggas die so others can live, and—in his mind—this brother will, especially after hearing about all of the money this cat had in his home.

"Does he have a family?" Spizz asked.

"Unfortunately, yes. Hopefully they are not around, but if they are, then I must kill them, too," Silence responded.

Spizz regretted he even asked.

Spizz was uncomfortable with how easy it was for Silence to murder women and children, but Silence said it was best that way and had always made it clear that no witnesses will be left behind!

Who was Spizz to argue with that? I mean, he knew what Silence was into and how he did things, but he offered his assistance every time.

"We have to find a hardware store," Silence said, breaking the silence in the room. "I have to cut off his hands before I kill him; Julio wants him to feel pain," he continued.

"So, does he want any of the nigga's money?" Spizz asked curiously, wondering how much of this fortune he would have to give up and how much he will be able to keep.

"No, but I will give his wife a percentage. I owe Julio that much," Silence replied.

Like most jobs, Silence did not care for what his victims had, but in this particular case, he only wanted enough to make sure that Julio and his wife were take care of. When it is all said and done, it will be as if he performed the hit for free, and for an old friend. He had no problem doing that.

"I respect that," Spizz replied, feeling the fact that his brother had strong morals and was very loyal beyond belief. "So, how long do you think we will be out here?" Spizz asked, thinking about the business he had back home.

"As long as it takes," Silence responded.

CHAPTER

10

Back home . . .

Fresh took Rican out of town to meet his man, so he could move some of the work he had. The hood was still on fire, so the show had to go on the road.

Rican was reluctant, but he left Rozay to tend to the hood. He also gave him the info he got from Fresh about the nigga Tok. He knew he can count on his little brah, but he also knew how hotheaded Rozay was.

"Aido. What's good, my boy? This Rozay. I wanna kick it with you about a situation we both need out of our way."

Rozay and Aido went back a few years. They used to put in work together doing home invasions together with Aido's other man, Tweek.

Tweek got killed about a month ago. Word got back that the nigga Casanova from out in the boarder had his hands in on that. Tweek was getting money out their way. He had the blocks pumping something crazy and it was cutting into Casanova pockets, so he sent his shooters after Tweek; they killed him and the bitch he was with.

Casanova and Paco were like brothers. They pretty much ran their side of town and would kill anybody who stood in the way.

"Yeah, I'm in the hood now," Rozay continued. "Meet me in the first," he said before hanging up.

Rozay knew where Paco and Casanova would be that night, thanks to Fresh. There was a baby shower at the community center for Tok's baby's mom. Most of the heavy hitters from their squad would be there as well. Rozay planned to take them all out that night, but it wouldn't be easy.

Aido and Rico sat on the porch, watching all of the hood traffic while smoking a blunt. Aido was thinking about the phone call he just got from his longtime friend and wondered what it could be about.

With everything that was going on, he just wished that his family was complete. Things have not been the same without Tweek, and he regretted not being out there with him when that shit went down; he thought maybe he could have changed the outcome.

"I miss that nigga," Aido finally said while passing the blunt to Rico.

"Yeah. I do, too. Shit is definitely different now, but I would feel a lot better if we knew how to find them niggas. That shit bothers me, kid."

"I know," Aido replied. "Hold shit down for a few hours. I gotta go holla at Rozay about something."

"You good?"

"Yeah. You know that's brah. He wants to bring something to my attention. If I need you I'll let you know."

—⁂—

As Aido pulled up around the hood, he didn't see Rozay, so decided to text him to let him know he was there. A few minutes later, he came out of one of the trap houses. He walked toward Aido's cream-colored XJ8 Jaguar and hopped in.

"What up, my goon?" Rozay said, showing his boy some love.

"Same situation. Money and murder."

"Speaking of that, I know where they fuck boys will be at tonight. Word is that the whole squad gone be out. Well, at least the ones we looking for," Rozay continued.

"The nigga Paco's baby mom is having a baby shower at the center, the one by the high rise on Mediterranean Ave."

"All we gotta do is post up and wait for the niggas to get there or catch them walking out; either way, them cats die tonight."

Aido sat there thinking about finally being able to get revenge for his brother Tweek, and it put a smile on his face.

"They really gone do that shit in our city," Aido asked, kind of confused as to such boldness, especially with them knowing that the niggas they were beefing with were a few blocks from where they would be at.

"Either niggas are on some cocky disrespectful shit thinking niggas is soft, or they just didn't think it all the way through. Either way, I'm riding. So what's up?" Rozay replied.

Rozay saw this as a chance to prove to Silence and Spizz that he can handle the hood just as well as Rican, if not better. So, any chance he gets to murder to set an example, then murder it is. And he knew taking out these two men would dismantle the boarder's whole operation.

"Let's do this. I'ma go talk to Rico about this to put him on board. He needs to be here, and I'll meet you back here. Wait, what time does the shit start?"

"Six o'clock."

"Aight. I'll be back 'round four, so we can put this shit together," Aido said as he let Rozay out and pulled out.

"This is gone be a long night," Rozay said to himself.

Meanwhile . . .

Tisha and her best friend, Monay, went on a little shopping spree, courtesy of Silence. Monay did not approve of her friend messing around with Silence. She thought that he was crazy and that one day he would hurt Tisha. Although he had never been violent towards her, Monay believed it was just a matter of time.

"So, where is your psychopath of a boyfriend," Monay asked in a very sarcastic way.

She knew how defensive Tisha was when it came to her man, but she still continued to throw shade whenever the opportunity presented itself.

"Stop calling him that, and he is out of town visiting family. Why does it matter to you?"

"Hmmm . . . Just asking, that's all. But I see you getting all red, so I'll drop it. Anyway, are you coming to my sister's baby shower tonight?

We having it at the center over by the lots where the courts used to be. I forgot the name of the street."

"Nah, I'll pass on that. It's not really my circle. I mean, I know you, but doesn't she mess with Paco?"

Tish knew the history with them Dominican niggas. Silence has never talked to her about it, but she had heard about the drama between his little homies and Paco's squad, so she saw no reason to betray her man for a baby shower.

"Yeah, but what does that have to do with anything?"

"It's just not my crowd, that's all," Tisha said. She thought about what Silence would say if he found out that she was there.

Around five that evening, Rozay, Aido, and Rico met up to go over their plans for that night. All three men were killers in their own right and they all had something to prove, so no matter who stood in their way, they would get the job done.

Parked uptown by the ocean plaza in a black Dodge Durango, they sat loading their guns as Rozay continued to speak.

"I doubt we will catch them going into the building—and that would be a bad idea anyway—being that they will most likely come in separate cars, at separate times. It's best that we wait for the exit."

"Why don't we just run up to the spot and catch those niggas off guard?" Rico questioned.

"It's a baby shower, and even though that is the case, them niggas are still in there strapped down, especially being that they are in our hood. The minute we bust through the doors, we could be the ones dead, not them. Besides, I know that is what they would expect."

"He's right, but that shit is wide open by the center. It is too much exposure my nigga", Aido added.

"Exactly, and that is why they chose that location, thinking we would be stupid to try something right there. Besides, I got it covered as to where most of the pigs will be when we murder these niggas. A couple of the little bros are downtown as we so speak, waiting for my text; and when they get it, a lot of shots will go off between Florida and Texas Ave. They will give us enough times to get low after rewards," Rozay said, reassuring his men that it will be a clean getaway.

"Say less. Now let's get this shit done," Aido spoke through clenched teeth.

They sat parked about a half block down and watched people go in and out of the center. Paco and Casanova were already inside. A few of their little niggas sat around the parking lot, smoking and keeping watch of their surroundings. Rozay and the squad were not at all worried about being out gunned because they had the element of surprise on their side, so at first the targets would not know what's going on or where the shots were coming from.

A few hours went by, and just as they saw a group of people dispersing from the center, Rozay sent the text to his team that was waiting downtown.

"Get ready, my niggas. Time to go duck hunting," Rozay said as he put the .50 round clip into his AR15. Rico and Aido were also armed with choppers; Rico had an M16 and Aido had a 100-shot Calico.

"There they go. Let's get it," Rico pointed.

As they got out of the car and ran up the block, Rozay let off a few rounds into the crowd of people where Paco and Casanova were standing. The first round hit Paco's pregnant wife in the stomach and the second caught her in the neck. People started to scream and began running back into the center.

Paco, along with his men, started to return fire in the direction where the shots were coming from. Rico crossed the street and ducked behind a parked car. He began shooting, hitting Casanova twice in the head and once in the chest.

Tok got the drop on Aido as he was crossing the street and tore a hole through his stomach and out on his back.

"Zay, Aido hit," Rico yelled while firing rapidly in an attempt to run and help his boy.

Rozay continued running up the block ducking behind cars while shooting in Paco's direction. Two of his men went down. You could see Tok limping while firing back, trying to get in his car.

"Bok, bok! Bok!" Shots rang back, hitting Rozay in his left shoulder.

"Fuck, I got hit. We gotta get the fuck out of here, my niggas. I hear twelve coming."

Rozay ran over to help Aido as he and Rico continue to fire, trying to hit everybody they could before speeding back to the hood.

"He's still breathing. We gotta hurry the fuck up before my nigga die. Drive to Philly," Rico instructed as they sped away from the crime scene.

Paco made it away with his life, only suffering from a leg shot, but in his eyes he might as well be dead. They just killed his unborn child and his baby's mother right in front of him. Not to mention Casanova, his right man. He knew it was a bad idea to throw the shower there, but it was the only place they could find within the time frame they had that was big enough.

Paco knew what he had to do, and knew he must act fast. He had never had a run-in with Silence, only his little man's, but he was well aware of who he was and knew that one day it would come to this. And that day was now.

Paco sped away, raging, with one thing on his mind: murder.

"Hello, Tish. Oh my god, they just killed Margret," Monay cried into the phone, hysterical from the event she had just witnessed. "She's dead. Niggas came through her fucking baby shower, shooting. A couple niggas are dead out front. I can't believe this shit just happened. These niggas was out here shooting for ten fucking minutes and the police are just getting here. Yeah I'm okay, but my mind is so fucked up right now. I'm not sure, but I think I saw Rozay little ass as I was running back into the center. It felt like he looked right at me," Monay continued.

"Okay, I'll call you when I'm on my way."

Tish sat on her bed, wishing she didn't hear what she'd just heard. She knew Rozay was her man's little homie, and if Monay put that out there that she thought she saw Rozay, then that could mean her friend's life. Either way, she has to tell Silence, because at the end of the day it affected him, too.

"Can things get any worse?" she asked herself as she began to text her man.

———m——

Rozay sped down the Expressway, hoping to make it there in time to save Aido. He was not worried about his own injury, because the bullet went in and out and didn't feel as if it hit any major arteries.

"Shit fucked up, kid. I don't think son gone make it," Rico said from the back seat while holding Aido's head in his lap.

"Not again. We've lost one; I can't lose you too, my nigga."

A few minutes later, Aido took his last breath.

CHAPTER

11

Back in Boston, 11 p.m.

Silence had been going over the plan with Spizz nonstop for the past twenty-four hours. He knew his plan was going to work, but it wouldn't be easy. Spizz, at this point, just wanted to get the job over with so he can see how much money he will come up with. Patience was not really his strong suit, not by a long shot.

"We've been watching this fucking crib all day, my nigga. When are we going to get this shit done?"

As usual, Silence sat there and ignored him. He knew how impatient Spizz was, and saw no point in entertaining the conversation. Finally, Silence noticed that Marco and his bodyguards were leaving his home, giving him the opportunity to put his plan in motion.

He figured it would be easier to get to Marco if they broke into his home while he wasn't there, so he waited.

"Let's go," he said as he and Spizz grabbed the bag they brought with them out of the back of the van.

The street Marco lived on was pretty dark. There were lots of trees surrounding each house, making it fairly difficult for a neighbor to see into your yard and the actual house.

Silence and Spizz ran through the yard, going towards the side of the house to disarm the security system sitting next to the fuse box. Neither one of them knew exactly how to disarm the alarm, but like everything else, you can learn how to do so on the internet.

Silence knew that Marco's family would be home, and usually he would have plans on killing everyone in the house, but Julio specifically said that his niece and nephew were to remain untouched. Julio didn't really care for Marco's wife, so Silence figured she must go as well.

"Once we are in, you grab his wife and I'll get his children; then we'll bring everyone back downstairs."

Spizz nodded in agreement, already aware of the plan. "Show time," Spizz said as they disarmed the system and headed for the back of the house.

Marco's family seemed to all be upstairs. Music could be heard playing from one of the kids' rooms. His son was the oldest; the daughter, from what they were told, had just turned fourteen.

As they approached the back patio, Silence pulled out a glass cutter for the sliding door that led into the kitchen. He cut out a circle and reached in to unlock the door. As they entered the house, they noticed that the layout was exactly as Julio said it would be, making it easier for them to navigate through the home.

"The wife's room is to the once we hit upstairs," Silence whispered as they headed towards the steps.

Once upstairs, Silence proceeded to the daughter's room as Spizz went for Marco's wife. Silence peeked in and noticed that the girl was asleep. Before going in, he looked down the hall, where the music was coming from to be sure that Marco's oldest boy was still behind his closed door.

Inside, Silence stood over the girl's sleeping body, looking for an angle in which he can grab her without giving the girl enough time to scream or make any sudden moves.

He took the rag he was carrying and quickly shifted her body so she was lying on her back. He then covered her nose and mouth with the rag, instantly putting her back to sleep. After tying her up, he left the room to do the same to her brother, this time using a gun to keep the kid in check.

Down the hall, Spizz already had Marco's wife tied up and gagged, so he went to the boy's room where Silence was waiting, as planned. They both knew the boy could be a problem, so decided to save him last.

"He must be in the bathroom," Spizz said, pointing out the steam coming from under the door.

"Then that makes it a whole lot easier," Silence replied as they both walked towards the bathroom door.

As Spizz pulled the shower current, both men raised their guns, scaring the boy so badly he slipped and banged his head on the side of the tub, knocking himself out.

"That was easy. Now let's tie this little nigga up," Spizz said while pulling the rope and tape from their bag. After tying up the son, they headed back towards Marco's bedroom where his wife was.

"Do you know where the money is?" Spizz asked the wife.

She nodded, so Spizz pulled the tape from her mouth and told her to speak.

"There is a safe in the back of my closet," the woman said. "Please don't hurt us. You can take the money. I know the code. Please, just take it and leave," she cried out.

After getting what he wanted, Spizz went into the closet where the safe was located and put in the code.

"Damn!" he said as he opened the safe and seeing stacks and stacks of money along with a gray .40-caliber with an extra clip.

Spizz started to stack all of the money into the other duffel bag he was carrying after putting the gun on his waistband.

Silence watched his accomplice drag the bag towards the bedroom door. "Take the bag downstairs and hurry back up, so we can move his family to the sitting area."

"Then what?"

Silence just stood there, ignoring the question before he finally answered. "We wait."

Back home

The city has been on fire since the shootout at the baby shower. Rozay and Rico were recovering from that night, both mourning of the loss of their friend, Aido. Both men knew that Silence and Spizz were going to be very upset about how the situation took place.

Silence had always said that if you were going to murder, then murder right; plan it to get away, not caught. Even they knew the whole thing was reckless.

"Rican is on his way back, and I heard Paco was putting some shit together for a war. You know that Fresh was fucking one of Paco's baby moms and she told him that the bitch Monay said it was us," Rozay said to Rico as they stayed in the trap house uptown.

"You think that bitch is going to the police?"

"Nah, I doubt it. She probably told Paco and he told the bitch to keep that quiet."

Rico lit up a blunt filled with weed laced in wet. Just the thought of not having his partner around anymore was enough to drive him crazy, and the mixture of these two drugs were going to make things even worse.

"I'm glad we killed his bitch and the baby, but that's not enough to ease my pain, brah. Before we kill him, I wanna murder everybody associated with him. Every spot he has, I'm going to blow them shits up. I'ma stop all this nigga's paper from coming in, make him suffer. Then he dies," Ricco ranted as the drugs began to take effect.

Rozay sat there nodding in agreement, but he knew Silence and Spizz were going to want to handle things their way.

"Tell Aido's family that I'll cover the funeral and let his baby mom know we're going make sure she good," Rozay said as he tried to call Silence once again.

Marco's home . . .

Silence and Spizz waited patiently for Marco to come back to his home. They could have easily made his wife call to speed things up, but this would have made him suspicious and put him on point, so they waited.

Marco's wife and two children were each tied to a chair. Sitting side by side at the kitchen table, across from them, were the two duffel bags of money Spizz took from the safe.

The family sat there surprisingly quiet, probably assuming they will live as they have not seen the men's faces and that the men have what they've come for.

"Three a.m. and still no Marco," Spizz said, looking at his custom Rolex.

Silence paid him no mind; he was reading the newspaper on the counter next to where Marco's family was sitting.

As Silence began to speak, they heard the front door open. Both men got into position to make their move. The way the house was set up was that there was a living room as well as a sitting area that separated the entrance and the kitchen, so Marco and his men were blind and had no clue what was waiting for them.

The man to the left of Marco was hit by the first shot and the second man, although caught off guard, jumped in front of Marco. He began to fire towards the area where the shots came from.

Silence hit the bodyguard in the back of the head as he walked around the foyer to creep up behind Marco and his men. Startled by what just occurred, Marco attempted to run back towards the front door.

"Not so fast," Silence said, pointing his gun at Marco's head. "You need to relax and go join the rest of your family in the kitchen."

"What the fuck is going on?"

"What does it look like?" Spizz said, appearing from the room in which he started shooting.

"You're about to die and your family is going to watch." Silence pushed the gun harder into his head, urging him to walk forward.

It made him smile to see such fear in a man who has betrayed his own family.

"Nothing is worse than dishonor," Silence said as they walked into the kitchen, where Marcos's family was bound.

"Don't you love family reunions?" Spizz cut in.

Not able to believe his eyes, Marco began to break down, begging these men not to kill his family. He saw the money on the table, so he knew they had what they came for.

Marco thought to himself, *Why are they still here?*

A masked Silence walked up to the side of Marco's wife and shot her twice. Blood flew; the others began to scream, which was not too loud since their mouths were gagged.

Marco sat their petrified, not able to move or say anything. Silence walked up beside him and whispered into his ear, not wanting his children to hear, "Your brother sent me."

Shocked at what he just heard, Marco began to get up to rush Silence. He stopped when he saw Spizz out of the corner of his eye point a gun at his daughter's head.

"Please, what do you want?"

"Your life, but first, your hands," Silence calmly said while pulling a machete out of the bag they brought with them.

"Put your hands on the table. You move them and he starts with the girl."

Shaking out of control, Marco complied with Silence's demands.

"Please don't hurt them," he got out before having his left hand cut off. "AUGGGGGGGGHHHHH!!!" Marco screamed before passing out from the pain.

Silence then placed Marco's right hand on the table, as the man was still passed out, and then cut that one off as well. This woke him back up, and he let out a menacing scream before being silenced with a shot to the head.

"Get the money. Let's go," Silence said as he placed Marco's hands in a bag and then headed for the door, leaving the children behind still tied to their chairs.

After leaving the scene, the two men went back to their hotel room to count the money. Silence promised himself to give Julio's wife a percentage of what Spizz took. He himself did not want any of it. The thrill of murder was by far enough to satisfy him; he just wanted to right a wrong.

Counting up all of the money, they realized how much it really turned out to be.

"Eight million, my nigga. You sure you don't want none of this?" Spizz asked in disbelief.

"Nah, just a piece for Julio," Silence replied as he turned his phone back on and read a text from Tish.

"Family emergency. We gotta get back," Silence said.

"I got a few missed calls and messages from Rozay saying the same shit."

The men packed up what they came with, but first they put aside a million dollars for Julio. Then they headed for the airport for their flight back to the city.

CHAPTER

12

Rican made it back in town sooner than he expected. He had no problem moving all of the dope he had; he just wished he had taken more. The situation that had just occurred needed his immediate attention.

He knew Rozay would do something stupid, but he didn't think it would be of this magnitude. Paco was a major problem for him, but Rican wanted to do things smartly, quietly, and with as little casualty as possible.

Fresh drove as Rican continued talking on the phone with Spizz. They were almost in the hood when they spotted Rico pulling out.

"Beep the horn," Rican directed, trying to get Rico's attention before he could go.

"Yo, what up, big brah?" Rico said when he noticed Fresh's navy blue Jaguar XJ8.

"Back up and park," Rican yelled out of the driver's side window.

Rican wanted both Rozay and Rico to be around when Silence and Spizz showed up, plus he himself wanted to know what the fuck actually happened and why they acted without approval.

As the men parked their cars, Rozay walked up after receiving a text from Rican saying he was outside.

"Fresh, what's good, brah. Haven't seen you since I been home. I see things shit change," he said as he approached his friends.

"Yeah, I'm Gucci, my nigga. Sucka ducking as usual. You know how it go. But I'ma leave y'all to it. I know y'all have some shit to discuss, but we definitely are going kick it once y'all handle business," Fresh said, giving peace to Rican and Rico before hopping in his whip to head back his own way.

"So tell me exactly what happened, and start from the beginning," Rican said as they walked over to a nearby porch where no one could hear them.

Silence's spot

As he approached his front door, Tish was already there waiting to jump into his arms. She was used to her man being gone for days at a time, but nobody can get used to the danger that comes with it. Whenever Silence went out of town, she prayed not to receive a call stating the worst about something happening to her man.

Tish had already lost her brother, and to lose Silence would be something she could possibly never get past.

"I missed you, baby," Tish said with tears in her eyes as she hugged and kissed Silence.

"I missed you more, but this affection has to wait. At least for the moment. So tell me what you know."

"Well, some guys shot up Monay's cousin's baby shower, killing her and the baby. Also, some guy was killed. I don't know who they are, but . . ."

"But what?"

"Monay said she saw Rozay shooting that night," Tish said with her head down.

Knowing what Silence was all about, she feared for her friend, but she loved her man.

Silence sat there for a moment, stuck in his thoughts. He understood the friendship the two women shared, but he knew what he needed to do—and that was kill Monay and everyone close to her she could have possibly told.

"I told her not to mention it to anybody," Tish assured him.

She knew he would kill Monay, and it hurt her deeply knowing it had to come to that, but keeping that information away from him could come to haunt her in the long run. So, she did what was best and now all she can do is mourn yet another loss. This time, it will be her best friend.

Silence kissed her on the forehead and told her he had to go.

"Come back to me!" Tish called out as she watched Silence get into his Porsche Panamera.

"Don't I always," he responded as he drove off and headed to the hood.

Back around the way

Spizz made a few runs before meeting up with his little homies. He had a lot of money around the city and not to mention the stop made to put up the seven mil he got off Marco. Things were truly going well for him and Silence. In his mind he couldn't for the life of him figure out how his partner could pass up on all of that paper.

He knew Silence was stacked up, not only because of the many jobs he gets, but because Silence was extremely smart. He was heavy into real estate and also played around with the stock market, but to pass up on millions was crazy.

As he pulled up around the hood, he got out and kicked it with a few youngins that were running around. After talking to them for a few minutes, he peeled off some paper for their pockets and continued on his way to meet up in the trap spot with his men.

Walking into the trap house, he was met by a cloud of weed smoke, followed by the flow of fiends running in and out. As he entered the kitchen, he saw Rican, Rozay, and Rico sitting around a makeshift table in the corner right next to the back door, discussing the events from the night before and what went wrong.

"I know where y'all lil niggas went wrong. Y'all didn't use ya fucking head. Y'all acted out of impulse instead of pure logic," Spizz said as he walked into the kitchen. "Whose call was this?"

"It's on me," Rozay answered.

"And where were you?" Spizz asked Rican, as he was left in charge of the affairs of the hood.

"I was O.T., moving work," Rican replied.

Rican and Silence were like family, and Spizz trusted him 100% when it came to handling and holding up what they have built, but he knew the situation with Tok would be too much for them.

"Where's Silence?" Rican asked, curious as to why the other mentor wasn't there.

That night

Silence was on his way to the next country over to bury Monay's body. He kidnapped her from her home after leaving Tish and changing his clothes.

Monay had just finished food shopping and had several bags in her hand. As she put the key in the door, she never heard Silence creep up behind her. When she did, it was too late.

Where she lived in the city was very quiet and she had several bushes surrounding her property, so that was perfect for what Silence had planned. After knocking her out, Silence tied her up with zip ties and threw her into trunk, where he had a shovel and chain saw.

He knew he could not let Monay live. She ran her mouth far too much and that could bring a lot of unwanted heat his way. Silence didn't approve of what went down—well, as least how it was done. Everyone knew that murder to him was like brushing his teeth, but reckless shooting was just not what he was into. His motto was to get the intended target and to make it personal.

Silence kept holes dug up in certain parts of South Jersey as a means to, of course, hide bodies, but he only did this to people he didn't want to be found. In this case, it was Monay, his wife's best friend.

As he drove down the long path that stretched deep into the woods, he lit a blunt and smiled at the thought of ridding the world of more evil. In Monay's case, it's being nosey and running her mouth.

About a half mile back, Silence finally stopped the car and got out to open the trunk. Once the truck was open, he saw Monay squinting her eyes, trying to see who was behind her abduction and why.

Once she realized it was Silence, she couldn't believe it. *Why would he do this?* she thought to herself.

Silence then pulled her petite frame out of the car and dragged her about thirty yards into the woods, where a hole was already dug out.

"Why are you doing this?" she cried out.

Like a madman, he ignored her cries. As they got close enough to her future grave, Silence stopped and started the chain saw.

"Please," was all she got out before Silence began to cut away at her body.

After dismembering and burying her, he got back in his car and drove to his next destination.

Back around the way

Rican and Rozay sat outside one of Paco's main trap spots dressed in all black. In the back seat of the car, they had a few bottles of gasoline with half a rag soaking inside and the other hanging out, and an AK assault rifle with a fifty-round magazine.

They discussed this plan with Spizz as a means to draw Paco out of hiding and to somewhat avenge Aido's death. Rico and another one of the youngins from the hood were a few blocks down with the same exact plan in motion.

They still were not sure where Silence was or what he was doing, but they wished he could be around to help.

"You ready, my nigga?" Rican asked Rozay as they both pulled the mask they were wearing over their faces. "Let's get it," Rozay simply replied.

As they exited the car, Rican came around and lit both bottles Rozay was holding. Immediately after, he tossed both bottles into the trap house windows.

A few seconds went by before the front door opened and men started to disperse, trying to get out of the house that was now in flames.

Directly in front of the house, armed with an assault rifle, Rican shot and killed every man that exited the trap just as they planned.

Smoke them out and gun them down.

At that very moment, Rico and the youngins were executing Paco's men the same way.

After killing everything in sight, the killers jumped back in their cars and headed back to the city.

Meanwhile

After getting rid of Monay, Silence decided to take care of the problems his little homies couldn't handle, which was Paco. Silence knew of him and was aware of the war that went on with him and his crew, but he stayed back to see how his protégés would handle the situation; and so far he didn't like it.

Silence felt as if the job wasn't done fast enough, so now he felt the need to intervene.

He knew exactly where Paco was hiding out; Monay told him before he killed her. He was a few towns away, about twenty five minutes outside Atlantic City, at his mother's house with three of his men standing guard.

Silence didn't see going alone a problem because he had dealt with situations like these quite a few times in the past and knew just what to do.

Paco had a man in the front of the house and one guarding the back. The third man stayed close to him inside his mother's house, so part of Silence's job was done for him: divide and conquer.

Being extremely light on his feet and dressed in all black, Silence blended into the night as if he was a part of it. Armed with a P95 nine-millimeter handgun with a silencer, he moved quickly and quietly towards the guard placed in front of the house.

The man was looking down at his phone while holding a gun in his other hand. Silence leaped over the gate, shooting him twice in the head before he could make a sound alerting anyone else that there was an intruder on the property.

Silence then proceeded to the back, creeping alongside of the house like a shadow in darkness.

As he approached the backyard, he peaked around the corner to get a clear visual of where the other guard was standing. Seeing him leaned up against the home, smoking a cigarette and not paying any attention to his surroundings, gave Silence the opportunity to strike.

As quietly and as quickly as possible, Silence hit the corner and aimed his weapon. The guard saw his reflection out of the corner of his eyes, but it was too late. One shot hit him in the middle of his forehead and came out of the back of his skull, splattering his brain all over the window he was standing next to.

Silence peeked through the back door that led into the kitchen and noticed Paco's mother in there washing dishes. Paco could be seen with his legs propped up on the table, talking on his phone, but his other guard couldn't be seen from where Silence was standing.

He then took a few steps back to look for an upstairs window he could climb into. He spotted one that was slightly cracked just above the kitchen.

The way the home was set up made it easy for Silence to climb onto the next level. He pulled the chair on the back patio at the back of the house, stood on top of it, and then jumped, hanging off the ledge of the roof.

Pulling himself up, he looked into the window to be sure no one else was around. Once he saw it was clear, he lifted the window and climbed in very quietly.

The television could be heard from downstairs. From where he was inside the house, nobody seemed to be up there. He crept along the wall that led toward the steps before stopping to see if he could see any moment downstairs. As he got closer to the bottom, the wall that separated the two-story home ended. Silence could now see into the living room where Paco was sitting. His guard was on the recliner, sound asleep, as Paco continued to talk on his phone.

Some guard! Silence thought to himself as he reached the bottom of the stairs undetected.

As he took his last step, he fired a shot into the sleeping guard's chest. Paco turned around immediately and was met with his own shot to the head.

"Good night," he said as he proceeded to the kitchen where his mother was still washing dishes, unaware of what just happened.

With her back turned to Silence, the last thing she saw before she died was the plate she just stacked on top of the shelf as Silence shot her in the back of the head.

CHAPTER

13

The next day

Spizz called a meeting with his young boys to discuss future plans about the Paco situation and the expansion of his drug empire. He figured since his come up, it was time to take things a little further, starting with the spot O.T. that Rican was telling him about. But first they had to finish the removal of a certain obstacle.

They met at a restaurant in the Tropicana called P.F. Chang's. Spizz and Rican were already there and have ordered their meals. Rico and Rozay have yet to arrive and Silence was still missing in action. He picked this spot not only because the food was good, but also because the setting was dimly lit and each booth was sectioned off from every other patron inside the establishment.

"I liked how y'all handled that job last night. It went exactly how it was supposed to go," Spizz said between bites.

Usually he was not the one to orchestrate a hit, but since Silence was not around and the situation needed to be addressed, Spizz stepped up.

"Yeah, it went really smooth, but I want the nigga, Paco," Rican replied.

In his eyes, this beef had gone on for far too long and the sooner Paco died, the sooner they can get the block back to the way it was.

"Here, these little niggas go right here," Spizz said, looking up to see Rozay and Rico walking up their table.

Before meeting at the restaurant, they decided to go past one of Paco's spots to maybe catch him out there and finish what he started. But news broke and now they had to tell the squad.

"They found Paco, his mom, and three other niggas dead at his mom's spot out the way a few minutes ago," Rozay said as he slid into the booth.

"Word. Somebody beat us to it," Rico added.

Spizz sat there for a moment, taking in what he was just told. He knew Silence was the one who took Paco out and figured that was the reason he hadn't been answering his phone. Silence never tells anyone, including Spizz, what he was up to. Even after it was done, he kept it to himself.

"HHMM . . . Well, that made things a lil easier, but I was hoping to get to this nigga personally," Rican said. He smiled to himself knowing who was really behind the hit.

Meanwhile, just a block away

B-Boy and one his closest business partners posted up in a motel room, discussing plans on getting into the drug market in the inner city. These men have the coke game on lock in New York and wanted to expand.

Silence was really what brought them to the area, but they couldn't seem to get to him, and everybody was too afraid to point him in the direction where they could find him.

"A, yo, son. This shit sweet down here. All these fucking tourists walking up and down this strip spending straight paper. We can turn this shit upside down, kid," Hollywood said.

B-boy was looking out of the room window to see all the traffic coming and going from different rooms where they were staying.

"Yeah, this situation does look good, but we gotta remember that this is not home, and we gotta do a lot of homework before we just open up shop; you know, figure out who is who, and most importantly build the trust and a team out of a few cats from down here. Treat them right, they treat us right; but first we gotta find this nigga, Silence. It's like he's a fucking ghost or a myth or some shit," B-boy said, expressing his frustration about not getting in contact with the man that brought him to this city.

"Say we find this nigga, you think he gone take the job?" Hollywood asked.

"Half a mil, I'm pretty sure that he would. Besides, that is what he does," B-Boy continued.

"Where the fuck is this nigga at?" he asked as they waited for a man who said he could contact Silence for a fee.

"I don't know, but do you trust him?" Hollywood asked.

"No choice at the moment," B-Boy said just as there was a light knock at the door.

"You looking for me?" Silence asked the man who opened the door. He was holding two .40-caliber Desert Eagles.

Silence had received a call earlier that day from one of his youngins saying some cat from New York was asking around about him and that his young boy would go to their room to discuss his whereabouts, so Silence decided to show up himself. If things looked funny, he planned on killing everyone there.

"No need for those," B-Boy said calmly with his hands raised, as he saw the guns Silence was holding.

"I'm here strictly for business purposes, nothing more," he continued.

Guns still in his hands, Silence stepped in and closed the door behind him. He noticed another cat sitting at the table, gripping his guns as well. He aimed at both men, preparing to shoot.

Seeing this, B-Boy told Hollywood to put his guns away and then he assured Silence that this was business and there was no need for weapons. Silence eased up a little after seeing Hollywood tuck his guns, so he did the same.

Still standing and curious about what this man wanted, he finally spoke, "Who are you, and who sent you?"

"A close associate of mine mentioned your name and services, and I need them," B-Boy replied.

Silence stood there studying B-Boy and his partner for a few minutes. He knew niggas be on some setup police shit, so he was always a little curious with whom he did business.

"I see the concern. I mean, I would be, too. Having some random nigga asking you to handle something for him . . . so take your time. I'm sure you have contacts around my way; do your homework and when you're satisfied, you know where to find me," B-Boy said.

Silence nodded his head and walked out of their motel room after telling him he'd be in touch.

"If you are not who you say you are, you will die before you make it out of my city," he said coldly before B-Boy closed the door behind him.

Back at the restaurant

The men sat and enjoyed their meal as they discussed plans on taking over the dope game in South Jersey. Spizz already has his hands all throughout their county and a few towns in the next county over. Now wished to make his operation bigger.

"So, tell me about that spot," Spizz said to Rican in between bites.

"It's out in Camden County. Niggas are about the paper, so they are not questioning who we are as long as we got the best work and better prices than what they are paying. I met a few of them cats, and they moving them things like a brick layer," Rican replied.

"I have to go down and meet with my plug to discuss a few things, and when I get back out that way. Rozay, I'm to send you out to Cape May. I got a few lil dudes out there that has been copping heavy, but it's already cats out there setting up shop. We are going to push them out. Rico, I want you out in Salem," Spizz continued. His phone began to ring.

"Hello."

"Yeah, I'll see you in a minute."

"That was Silence. I gotta get with brah, but after I talk to the plug we are going to have another sit down to finish this conversation. In the meantime, I had 1,500 bricks dropped off at the spot in the hood while he were here, so handle that. I'll pick up the rest of that paper tomorrow," Spizz said as he gave everybody dap before leaving out to meet up with Silence.

He called Spizz to have him meet up at their spot—to finish what he had started.

Monay had lived at the home where Silence kidnapped her with her twin sister, Shanice. He knew they were pretty tight and that Monay probably confided in her about what she saw that night, so she had to go as well.

As he pulled on the side of the house, he noticed that Shanice was there because the white Acura she often drove was parked out front. Getting in would not be a problem for him at all, being that she had been trying to give him the pussy for years. He would use that to his advantage. Shanice was inside, making herself dinner, when she heard a knock on the back door.

"Who is it," she asked.

"Silence."

Shanice opened the door with no hesitation. She figured he had finally come to his senses and decided to give her some of that dick.

"So, what do I owe this surprise?" she asked as she opened the door for him to come in.

"Where's your sister?" he questioned.

"Knowing her, she is cooped up in some nigga crib, playing house," she responded.

"You hungry?"

"Sure, why not," Silence responded as he walked over to the kitchen table, careful not to touch anything.

Silence figured he would see she knew before he killed her, see if she had told anybody anything—if she even knew.

"I'm sorry about your cousin," he said, referring to the shootout at the baby shower.

"Thank you. I wasn't there that night. I had to work, but Monay told me about it though."

"They still don't know who did it," Silence asked.

"Nah, the police don't, but Monay said she saw Rozay. I heard they found Aido's body in Philly. I don't know if that has something to do with anything."

"What do you think?" he questioned.

"I don't know what to think, but I kept my mouth shut about the Rozay thing 'cause I know that he was one of ya young boys," she quickly replied after seeing Silence tense up.

"Relax, baby girl. We good. Now, let's eat."

As they were eating the spaghetti and garlic bread she had prepared, Shanice asked Silence when were they going to fuck.

"Now," Silence responded.

He shot her in the head from across the table. There wasn't much noise because of the silencer he had attached to his 9mm. After killing her, he sat and enjoyed the rest of his meal. He took the plate, fork, and glass he drank from as a means of not leaving any DNA behind.

While Spizz waited for Silence to show up at the spot, he figured that he could use some entertainment while waiting behind the wheel of his pearl-white Escalade. He called the project whore to keep him company.

Jasmine was one of the baddest bitches Spizz had ever seen, but he could never take her seriously on the account of her past. She was 5'7", 140 pounds, all ass, slit waist, smooth chocolate complexion, and lips that would drive a nigga crazy.

"Jaz, what's up, baby girl?"

"Nothing. Same shit. My stupid-ass baby daddy on some bullshit with my son talking about he want a fucking blood test. My son is four years old and now he wanna trip over a blood test," she vented.

Spizz just sat there, not really giving a fuck about the situation. He just wanted his dick sucked.

"You get what you ask for Jaz. You know your lifestyle and how niggas look at you, so stop fronting like the victim and come over here and put this dick in ya mouth," Spizz said while unzipping his pants.

"I can't stand you, Spizz. You get on my fucking nerve, but you are lucky I like the way your dick tastes or I wouldn't let you talk to me that way," she said as she leaned down and started sucking Spizz's dick as if the shit was going out of style.

Jaz was a professional when it came to sucking dick, and for this reason alone is why Spizz has never fucked her. He heard that the pussy was garbage and all beat up, so he opted for the better part of her body.

She sucked away, slurping, spitting, and swallowing. Spizz reclined the seat back to get a better angle.

"Oh, shit. Damn bitch," he moaned as he pushed her head further down until he felt the back of her throat.

Jaz sucked his dick for a good ten minutes before he exploded in her mouth. Being the professional that she was, she swallowed every drop and continued to suck even more, going for round two, until they were interrupted by a knock on the driver's side window.

"We gotta talk," Silence said as Spizz rolled the window down. He saw Jaz and told Spizz to finish up. He then he proceeded to the trap house to wait for Spizz.

"We'll finish later, here's $500 for your pockets."

In a way, he was glad Silence showed up because he got what he wanted and he knew Jazmine wanted to fuck. That is why she kept going even after he nutted all in her mouth.

"You better call me this time, Spizz," she said as she exited the car.

Silence waited inside the trap house for Spizz to walk through the door. He lit his blunt and then decided to call Tish to make sure she was cool. Before he could dial her number, Spizz walked through the door.

"I met with the cat B-Boy about an hour ago," Silence said in between puffs of his weed.

"Why didn't you call me?" Spizz asked; he thought about the situation going wrong if B-Boy was on some bullshit.

"He needs my assistance," Silence replied, completely ignoring the question.

"So, now what?"

"We go up top to get info on this nigga."

Silence knew quite a few official cats in New York that he trusted, so he planned to go up there to do his homework on B-Boy before making any commitments. A phone call would be easier, but he tends to stick to the old-school rules of meeting face to face.

"Did you hear about the nigga, Paco?" Spizz questioned, already knowing it was his friend that put in the work.

"Yeah, I heard. We leave in the morning," Silence said as he left Spizz to his own thoughts.

CHAPTER

14

A lot of Tish's time was spent at the hospital where she worked. She pretty much used that as a means of not worrying so much about Silence. She has been working there for the past nine years, seven of which were spent taking classes to be where she is today.

Tish started off as a registered nurse and, as time went on, she found a sudden interest in being a surgeon; so Silence convinced her to follow her passion.

"Dr. Rose, please come to the front desk. There are people here to see you," the hospital clerk announced loudly over the intercom.

"What is it now?" Tish asked herself.

She left her office to head downstairs towards the front desk. She didn't get too many visitors at her job; in fact, she didn't receive any.

This is an unexpected visit and can only mean bad news, she thought to herself as she approached the front desk and see two detectives waiting for her.

"Hello, Ms. Rose. I am Detective Stevenson and this is my partner, Detective Scott. We're from the homicide department and we would like to ask you a few questions. Do you have somewhere private where we can talk?"

Thrown off guard and growing particularly nervous, Tish directed them to the conference room located just down the hall.

"What is this pertaining to?" she asked as they enter the small room.

The detectives looked at each other before telling her to have a seat.

Tish had never been in the same room with the police before, let alone be questioned by them, but Silence had gone over scenarios like this to prepare her for it just in case.

"Do you know a Monay Brown, Ms. Rose?" Detective Scott questioned.

"Yes. She is my best friend. What about her?"

"Well, she has been missing for quite a few days now and we would like to know when was the last time you spoke with Ms. Brown?" Detective Stevenson cut in.

Tish was well aware of her friend's disappearing acts. Whenever she met a new guy, there was a good chance she would be somewhere playing house, so not hearing from her was quite normal, she explained to the detectives.

"I'm sure she will pop up in a few days. This is nothing new. As a matter of fact, it is classic Monay."

"You see, that is the same thing her family has said, but I find it a little strange to have found her twin sister murdered in their home and now 'she' is missing," Detective Scott replied.

Tish began to worry about her friend and was speechless about what the detectives just told her about Shanice, Monay's twin sister.

"I don't know anything about that. Like I said, me not hearing from Monay is pretty normal, but now I am starting to worry," Tish said with a look of concern on her face.

"Are you still involved with Silence Jihad?" Detective Stevenson asked as he looked into the file he was carrying with him.

"What does that have to do with anything, and how do you know that?" Tish replied, now getting a little defensive after hearing her man's name.

"People talk. And they said Monay was there when her cousin was murdered along with a few other people the night of the baby shower. And word is that Silence's people had something to do with the hit. We are still investigating, but things are pointing in his direction," Detective Scott said, trying to convince Tish they knew exactly what they were talking about.

Silence had taught her the deception game the police use to get information, so she was well aware of the fact they were fishing, but she played along as if she had no clue.

"Well, I have no idea what you're talking about. Yeah, I have heard; people do read the newspaper and it was all over the news, but I can assure you that Silence had nothing to do with that. He is a business man and left the streets alone long ago," Tish said in defense of her man.

The detectives began to whisper things to each other before speaking again. They knew she was protecting Silence because her body language said so and they were trained to read things of that nature.

"We know exactly what Silence is involved in. The only thing that keeps him out on these streets is the fact that he kills everyone he expects will talk and give him up. The properties and whatever else he has going on is just a front for guys like us. He's a fucking killer—you know, we know, and trust me . . . we will put these pieces together, and when we do, you will also go to jail for hindering the apprehension of a felon. Do you want that to be your future?" the detectives said, in another attempt to get some kind of information out of her.

"Are you guys here to talk about my missing friend, or to ask about my boyfriend?" Tish asked sarcastically, growing tired of the questions.

"We are talking about your missing friend. We believe Silence killed her sister and then took her somewhere and killed her as well!" Detective Scott said, beginning to get frustrated with Tish.

"Well, I do not know anything. I haven't spoken to Monay in a few days and therefore I can be of no help to this investigation. Now, if you will excuse me, I have to get back to work," Tish said before leaving the detectives stoned-faced in the conference room as they watched her disappear down the hall.

"She knows something," Detective Scott said to his partner as they exited the area where they were questioning Tish.

"Soon we will find out, and when we do . . . she goes right down with him," Stevenson responded as they left the hospital.

As Tish got back to her office on the second floor of the hospital, she pulled out her phone to text Silence what just happened.

Detectives just came to my job asking questions, read the text.

Waiting for a response, she began thinking about what the detectives have just told her. Part of her knew the truth and, as much as she loved Monay, she could not find it in herself to turn in the love of her life. All that she could do at this point was move on and stand by her man, no matter what happened.

"I trust that you stood your ground, and we will talk when I get back in town," was what Silence texted in return.

Tish sat back everything that has been going on.

"This is the life I signed up to be a part of, so I must stick by my man," she said to herself as she went to prepare for the surgery that was scheduled for that afternoon.

Meanwhile

Rican and Rozay had been working nonstop to get the block back to jumping the way it used to be before the heat came. Not only have they teamed up with Rico to form an alliance where they would control much of the midtown and uptown area, but they also sent a few young boys from the hood to take over the downtown area as well.

Downtown is where the out-of-town niggas get their money. That has always been a neutral zone when it came to getting money, but Rican wanted it all.

Not only were they dealing in and around the city, but he had also sent 500 bricks to Fresh's man in Camden as a means of keeping the spot open for him once Spizz gets back to him about the expansion.

"You think them boarder cats will try to get back at us for Paco?" Rozay asked Rican.

They were sitting on one of the project stoops, watching friends go in and out of the trap houses that were spread through the hood.

"They might, but they lost their backbone and now have no support. We can take our time killing the rest of them because, without Paco and Cas, them little niggas are nobody," Rican replied, not really caring too much about the situation.

"Speaking of Paco," you think big brah played his hands in that one?" Rozay asked, already knowing the answer to his own question.

Rican sat there for a minute thinking about the question. He had known Silence just as long as Spizz, but he was a few years younger than them. As the years went on, they stuck to each other like glue and in the process taught Rican the game along the way.

"Your guess is as good as mine, my G, but whatever the case maybe, it's done, so now we move on with it," Rican replied. "But what I do know is that the way Spizz is coming about this dope game, we are going to be on top and you already know that murder comes along with that, so be ready," he added.

Rozay nodded his head in agreement as one of their fiends approached them carrying a bag filled with household supplies.

"Hey, youngins, I got candles, air fresheners, toothpaste, body washes, you name it. I got it, and if I don't, then I'll get it!" he said, hoping to make a sale so he can get his afternoon fix.

"How much for the whole bag, old head?" Rican asked.

"For you, youngin, give me $40."

"Come on, O.G., get off ya bullshit. If I'ma spend that, I might as well go to the store myself," Rican replied, knowing the fiend was trying to get as much out of him as he could so he can get high.

"The money is going back in ya pockets anyway, youngin," the fiend said with a chipped smile.

"I'll give you $30—that's it, my man. These other little niggas ain't looking to be buying no fucking cosmetics off of you O.G., so go ahead and come off that. I know shorty can use it," Rican said.

"Aight, youngin. You got it," the man said as they exchanged money for the products.

"Next time, boost some clothes, jewelry, or some shit," Rozay said to the man as he walked off to the nearest trap house. "Whatever happened to that New York nigga that was out here looking for brah?" Rozay asked Rican.

"Don't know. Nobody has seen son since, and if they have, they haven't said anything," Rican replied, just as curious to know what happened to him as Rozay was.

CHAPTER

15

Silence and Spizz arrived in Brooklyn, New York, the following morning. As usual the men came prepared to do a job, being that eighty-five percent of the trips they took resulted in them putting in work.

Each of them drove in a separate vehicle—one to dump and one for the drive back home.

Silence drove a '96 Volvo, midnight blue with beige interior; in the trunk were rope, tape, and a few handguns along with an assault rifle, just in case.

Spizz drove not too far behind him in Silence's black Range Rover. They parked in front of a few townhouses down the block from where they were with a cat named Outlaw from the infamous Marcy project in Brooklyn.

Outlaw wasn't a drug dealer by any means. His lane was the stickups and home invasion, but he knew everybody when it came to N.Y. Whether it was Harlem or the Bronx, in his line of work, you had to be on top of the game.

Silence and Spizz exited their vehicles and walked up to where Outlaw was parked, which was a few cars up.

Outlaw was slouched back in a maroon BMW X5, smoking a blunt while cursing some bitch out on the phone. As the two approached the car, they heard him speaking through clenched teeth into the receiver.

"Bitch, I know what's going on. Ain't nothing slow about me but my walk!" he said before hanging up.

"You good, kid?" Silence asked as he slipped into the passenger side and Spizz slid in the back.

Silence met Outlaw at the Borgata down in Atlantic City a few years back. Outlaw got into it with some clown-ass cat named Maurice from a spot by A.C. called Pleasantville. Joel was the weed man in the area, but son was a tender bitch nigga when it came to them ho bitches.

Long story short, Outlaw was at the bar with the dude's baby mom, and the cat Joel tried to draw out and cause a scene. Outlaw clutched his hammer, not thinking twice of his surroundings. Silence peeped it and stepped in, pulling the stranger to the side.

"I don't know you, but anybody willing to bust they gun where they stand . . . I respect it! Son ain't worth it, though. He get a couple dollars, but he's no threat."

Afterwards, the two men got to talking, you know . . . about the average hood politics, line of work and things of that nature. Both men were feeling the way the vibes were in terms of recognizing real ones.

They stayed in contact after that night. Outlaw even went as far as killing some nigga for Silence to show good faith and that he meant business, so it was safe to say that Silence valued his word.

"Yeah, son, I'm straight. This silly-ass bitch got a nigga all out of his element, but that's another story. What did you have to holla at me about?" Outlaw responded with a look of curiosity.

Silence sat for a moment, thinking about the situation before answering. He didn't want to come off hostile in front of the man he had come to respect.

"Would you happen to know a cat named B-Boy?" he asked while looking Outlaw in the eye.

Outlaw leaned back into his seat and smiled as the named rolled off of Silence's tongue. He sat quiet for a minute, making Silence and Spizz a bit uncomfortable.

"I take it that you do?" Silence spoke in a serious tone, still looking at Outlaw.

"Yeah, I know him. Well, know *of* him. We have a bit of an unknown history, well, unknown to him, that is."

"So what can you tell me about him?"

"Besides the fact that I have been trying to get at the nigga for a few years now? Well, I done kidnapped, robbed, and killed a few of his people, but I can never seem to get to him. Son is stacked down."

Silence sat there taking in all that was said, but he needed more—like what did B-Boy want with him?

"He came looking for me, saying he needed my assistance. What do you make of that?" Silence asked.

"I've never known him to be a fuck nigga, if that is what you're asking, and as far as business goes, he's good on that note. But why he would need you for anything is a question mark for me because he has killahs," Outlaw responded.

The three men sat in silence, all deep in their own thoughts about the whole situation concerning B-Boy.

"Fuck, like I said, he does good business. After you conduct your business, feed him to me—and everybody leaves happy," Outlaw put out there, breaking the peace.

"If we do that, what will we get out of the deal on your end?" Spizz finally spoke up.

"I'll break off half," he replied reluctantly.

Silence sat in silence as he considered the proposal. Usually he would never be on board with something like that—robbing a customer. But Outlaw had murdered for him in the past and the favor was never returned, so this would make things even.

"We'll do it, but I'm not doing it for the money. I'm doing it to return the favor," Silence spoke as he looked back at Spizz.

"Aight, that's cool, but I still want to break y'all off with something 'cause, like I said, son is stacked! But there is something that can put us square?" said Outlaw.

Meanwhile, back home

Rican, Rozay, and Rico were carrying out the plans Spizz put into play as far as their positions in the drug game were concerned. Rozay was down in Cape May County, while Rican and Rico were posted up on the block between New York and Kentucky Ave. Both men put niggas in charge of the work they were responsible for both in Camden and Salem counties, so they had a little free time to kick it further about future plans.

"What's up with them spots out in the Ville?" Rico asked between the puffs from the Newport he was smoking.

The Ville was the next town over, where them boarder cats were moving all of their work.

"Without Paco and Cas, that shit is an open market, kid!" he continued.

"Without right. I wasn't even thinking about it. The only thing that came to mind when it came to the Ville was killing them bean-eating mothafuckers."

Both men shared a laugh as they thought of all the men they have murdered from the other side. As they continued discussing plans of taking over the boarder's territory, they never saw the black Dodge Magnum creeping up the block.

BOC, BOC, BOC, BOC . . . BRRRRRRRAT, BOC, BOC . . .

The masked men fired as they stopped in the middle of the street.

The first shot hit Rico in the back of his head, splattering his brain all over the side of Rican's face.

BRRRRRRAT, BOC . . .

Shots continued to ring as Rican jumped off the stoop and ducked behind the concrete stairs. He had his gun out but couldn't get a shot off because the bullets from the other end kept firing.

After about a minute or two, sirens could be heard in the distance. The car with the men was even louder as it sped off, rubber burning, and screeching from the sharp turns as they let a few more shots off.

Back in Brooklyn

Silence and Spizz climbed the back fire escape to an apartment building in downtown Brooklyn. Dressed in black, they blended in perfectly in the darkness of the alley that led them to where they were.

Outlaw wanted his best friend dead for going behind his back and fucking his wife of four years. He and Shadow had been childhood friends their whole lives, even committing all of their crimes together.

A few weeks back, one of Outlaw's youngins put him up on what was going on. First he couldn't believe it until just last night. He went through her phone and found messages of them going back and forth conspiring to kill Outlaw, so they can take all of his money and be together.

Just then, he knew he had to kill the mother of his child as well as his childhood friend, but he just couldn't find it in himself to do it.

As they approached Shadow's apartment, they saw that the house was dimly lit by candles and music could be heard playing from the living area.

"You go left, I go right," Silence directed as they climbed into the window leading into the kitchen.

The apartment was pretty typical. There were two entrances to the kitchen; one leading into the living room and another to the dining area. A bedroom down the hall and the bathroom a few feet away from the dining area.

Silence peeked around the corner leading into the living room. There he saw Shadow sitting on the couch, his head leaned back while getting his dick sucked by what looked to be a redheaded Redbone with a body anyone would kill for. Out of the corner of his eye, he noticed Spizz approaching, tiptoeing down the hall.

"SHHH!" Silence motioned while pointing towards the couch.

Spizz looked and shook his head, reading Silence's mind as to what to do next. Neither Shadow nor the unknown female heard anything due to the music playing and them being so into what they were doing.

Both men crept into the dimly lit area and fired one shot in each of their heads—Silence shooting Shadow and Spizz, the female.

They exited the house the same way they came in, leaving their victims in the same positions they were in before their death: Shadow leaning back with his dick in the bitch's mouth and she with a hole in the back of her head.

"You think that was Outlaw's bitch?" Spizz asked as they drove away from the crime scene.

"More than likely it was, but fuck it, loyalty is everything and if you break it, then you die . . . simple as that."

As they dumped the Volvo and got into Silence's Range Rover, Spizz cut his phone on to check on things back home.

"Cut ya phone on! I got hella text messages and voicemails, and a lot of them are from Rican!" Spizz said with a look of concern on his face.

Silence powered his phone up and saw he had just as many messages as Spizz, and all of them read the same thing: *RICO IS DEAD!*

"We gotta get back. Text Outlaw and let him know that it's done and that something important came up and what we talked about is a go. I'll get with him in the future with details," Silence said as they sped off in his Range Rover.

CHAPTER

16

Tisha and her friend, Courtney, sat on a park bench talking as they watched their children on the playground swinging from the jungle gym. It was the middle of summer, so they both couldn't wait to get out of the summer heat.

They ate strawberry icies that they bought just moments before Courtney started being nosy, asking about Silence as she often did.

"So how is the husband treating you?" she asked with a look of disgust on her face showing her disapproval of their relationship.

"We're not doing this today!" Tisha quickly responded, knowing where the conversation was headed.

Courtney never liked Silence because of just how much every opportunity she got.

"I just worry about you, that's all," she replied, still tight-faced at the thought of them being together.

Tisha ignored her friend and sat there in a daze as she watched her daughter playing, thinking back to the day she found out that she was pregnant.

"Congratulations, Ms. Rose, you're pregnant with a baby girl!" Dr. Patel said in excitement as if she were the one having a baby.

Tish sat in silence with a blank expression on her face, thinking about the future of her new baby girl. It wasn't that she was not happy, it was the fact that she felt a lil uncomfortable bringing a baby into this world with her baby's father being in the life he was in. She didn't want to be stuck raising a baby on her own.

"Is everything okay, Ms. Rose?" the doctor asked with a look of confusion on her face.

"I'm sorry, I just had no idea I was even pregnant. I mean, I'm not even showing. Don't you have to be a certain amount of months to even find out what the sex of the baby is?" Tish asked.

"Yes, that is very true and sometimes during a pregnancy you will not have any symptoms and, in rare cases, you will continue your monthly menstrual cycle. And to answer your question, you are thirteen weeks pregnant. I will start you on pre-natal vitamins right away and schedule another checkup weeks from today. Do you have any other questions?"

"No," she answered, still a bit surprised and overwhelmed by the news.

"Okay, I'll have the nurse come back and finish up this paperwork while I write you a few prescriptions for the vitamins." Dr. Patel said before leaving the room.

Tisha tried calling Silence to share the news, but the calls continued to go to voice mail.

"What am I going to do?" she asked herself.

She wanted nothing more than to have Silence's baby, but she wanted him to be there to help raise her. With how things were going out in those streets, she wasn't sure it would happen. But she was sure about one thing, and that was always keeping a part of Silence alive.

Around the way

Rican and Rozay sat patiently waiting for Spizz and Silence to arrive, so they can properly plan their next move.

"Damn, this shit hurts, my nigga. I mean, we winning, but we losing at the same time . . . I should have been more on point because if I was there, Rico would still be here!" Rican expressed as he replayed the moment when he watched Rico's brain come out of the front of his head.

"It's not ya fault, brah. I mean, them niggas will always be in our hearts, but niggas die everyday . . . so fuck all of that grieving shit. Let's get back," Rozay said as he stood on the porch staring at the memorial that was set up where Rico was gunned down.

The block was hot, but that didn't stop these men from handling business. There were patrol cars riding back and forth, and they even went as far as walking around the projects to make their presence known by all. Of course, nobody saw anything, making the Jakes' job that much harder, but fuck it.

"You're right, but we don't even know who the fuck came through blazing. I mean, the only problems we had was with them boarder niggas, and most they are in the dirt, so we have to figure out what is going on and who was behind it," Rican responded.

As they continued their conversation, Silence pulled up in a cream-colored Buick Enclave he had rented just hours after arriving back from New York. He sat behind tinted windows watching his two youngins off point again. They didn't know who was in the car and what the intentions were, especially since this was car they had never seen around before.

"Y'all niggas are slipping!" he yelled as he rolled the window down, finally catching their attention. "Let's go, get in."

Rican and Rozay walked over to where Silence was parked and were ready to jump into the wheels when they heard shots popping off from an assault rifle of some sort.

Two shots blew out the back window of the rental car. The men ducked, unable to tell exactly where the shots were coming from.

"Get in!" Silence said calmly while slightly ducking down in the driver's seat.

Rican and Rozay dove into the back seat as Silence pulled off recklessly, driving up the block and making a hard left towards these little projects not far from where they were.

"Who the fuck was that and where the fuck were they at?" Rican said, out of breath and a bit shaken.

Silence pulled into a parking lot across from this apartment building they also operated out of; they called it the school house.

"I guess it's true what I was told," Silence said as he began rolling up blunt and replaying in his head what just happened. "Paco has a big family out in Baltimore, and word is that a lot of them are out here for blood," Silence added as hit lit his blunt. "Be smart, calculate your movements, and always be on point. I'm with y'all on this. Nobody is exempt; anybody you see that is associated with anyone form the boarder . . . kill them all. Go to their homes, jobs, schools, or whatever. Everybody dies."

"This shit is getting thick big, brah. I mean, I don't mind because I love it and I like to beef, but they slowing our paper up with these wild cowboy shootings," Rican expressed, thinking about all of the work they have in the hood that they can't get to because the heat.

"Rozay, you good, lil brah? You kind of quiet back there," Silence said while looking through the rearview mirror at his two men.

"I'm good, big brah. I'm just calculating our moves because I plan on riding out tonight. I want to end this shit. This nigga is in the grave yet still causing us fucking problems," Rozay replied.

These men had no idea what was next to come. The Dominican cartel stretched deep along the East Coast, and Paco was one of their main suppliers—and not to mention he was family.

Paco's cousin from Baltimore was a killer at heart and he was just as good as Silence in the murder department. The only difference was that he was sloppy and reckless. Wherever he saw you, that was where he left you. They call him Deuce.

"Relax, lil brah. I'll take care of it. Spizz should be here any minute. Go up to Sheeda's crib and wait for my car. As soon as I get a location, I'll get it to y'all and then you can handle ya business . . . Remember . . . Protect what's yours!"

The men said their peace and went their separate ways, leaving in the air thoughts of murder.

As Silence pulled out of the parking lot, Spizz also pulled up in a rental car.

"What up, my goon? What just happened?" Spizz asked after seeing the back window blown out along with several bullet holes on the side of the rental.

"A few long-distance shooters, nothing major. But the lil bros are up in Sheeda's crib. I'm about to go kick with the cat B-Boy. But later on we have a lot to discuss," Silence said before pulling off, leaving Spizz trapped in his own thoughts.

Spizz knew it was another brewing, this one even bigger than the last one. He deeply hated times like these for the simple fact that it interfered with business, but he also knew that money and murder went hand-in-hand, so avoiding it when you're up . . . GOOD LUCK WITH THAT!

Spizz sat in the rental processing his thoughts for a few minutes before texting Rican and letting him know he was on his way up. There was a lot to discuss and little time to calculate. One thing for sure, he was ready.

"Murder is what it is when the money slows up."

CHAPTER

17

Silence met up with B-Boy in this hole-in-the-wall joint called Sweet Cheeks. He had been there for an hour before B-Boy arrived. The place was smoked out. Old heads playing pool in the corner while the bar was being occupied by some wannabe pimp niggas laying their weak shit down on some old drunk bitches.

Silence liked this environment for the simple fact that everybody minded their own business and if shit were to go down, they would be too drunk to even know what happened.

From where Silence sat, he could see everyone who left and came into the bar. While deep in thought, he caught a glimpse of B-Boy, so he zoomed in, paying very close attention to who came with him and what direction they went in—just in case this nigga was about to talk some dumb shit and had to get left.

As he approached, Silence leaned back in the chair he was sitting in and locked eyes with the man to see where his head was. You can easily spot a sucka. Yeah, he was told that B-Boy was an official goon, but sometimes you have to be your own judge of niggas . . . in case the last nigga missed something.

"What up, killa?" B-Boy said over the music as he extended his hand.

Silence never liked being called out of his name and hearing this switched his approach from chill to murder just like that.

"Silence!" he responded, leaving B-Boy's hands shaking the air. "Don't ever call me 'killa' again. You call me who I am and nothing more!" he continued sternly.

B-Boy raised his hands as a sign of peace while stating no disrespect. In the back of his mind, Silence counted this as a strike.

"Have a seat," Silence said. He was still a little tense about the situation, but he left it alone for potential business's sake. "So, tell me . . . what is it that you can't get done?" he asked as he leaned back in his seat and lit the blunt that sat in the table in front of him.

Music played in the background. It was an old head bar, so you know the type of music it played; it was just loud enough so no one could hear the conversation they were having.

"I need two men off of the map, these fuck-ass niggas . . ."

Silence waved him off, stopping the part about the details. "I don't need the why, just the who and where!"

"Silence—a man who lives by his name. The less, the better, huh?" B-Boy asked.

"Exactly. Now proceed!" He knew he was rubbing this New Yorker the wrong way; body language spoke that, but and soon, B-Boy will see just how about his business Silence truly was.

"Aight. One nigga lives out in Hoboken and the other out in Elizabeth. We did business together. Shit went south, and my hittas don't have the right resources to get close to these niggas, and that's where you come in."

"What are these two heads worth to you?" Silence asked in between puffs of his weed. He continued to maintain strong eye contact with this friendly out-of-towner.

"That's the thing, I want them and their loved ones out of the picture. Whole house wiped out!" B-Boy said while extending his arms out in a wide motion as a means to make his point clear.

Silence sat there for a minute or two, contemplating the situation and at the same time trying to read between the lines about the hand that was just laid in front of him.

"Fifty racks a head. I'll get with you with the calculations when it's done and I need a hundred grand up front for the two heads in question," Silence finally said as he deaded the dutch he was smoking.

"I can do that. I'm going to send you their names and pics. To ya phone," B-Boy said as he pulled out his iPhone.

"Nah, playboy . . . I don't do business like that! No phone, no text . . . Get my money along with the still prints of them niggas. Names on the back, and when you get that . . . hit me."

Silence said as he slid out of his seat, leaving B-Boy to ponder.

As Silence walked out of the bar, he approached a gray Challenger parked across the street directly in front of the bar.

As he approached, the passenger's side window rolled down, releasing a cloud of weed smoke that suffocated both passengers.

"That white Beemer . . . Stay on 'em! I want to know who these niggas know down here, where they go, and how many niggas are with him at any given time."

"Say less!" the driver spoke over the passenger as he rolled the window back up while watching Silence get in his Range and pull off.

Somewhere in the sticks

Rican and Rozay lay low out G-Way, a few towns away from the city. They had a bag up spot around these condos that Spizz set up for them. The community was gated, so intruders were the least of their worries. They had four white bitches staying there who went to Rutgers University. The men used them to bag up their work and sometimes went as far as using them as bait for any sucka who would fall into their trap.

"Amanda, I'm gone need you to make a drop for me out in Tom's River . . . You remember white boy Tommy that I introduced you to at Club Dusk a few months ago?" Rican asked as he read the paper about the shooting that took place the day before.

Amanda was by far his favorite. She was a redhead, about 5'7", real petite but her attitude was everything, and she took no shit from nobody. One could never tell at first glance how evil she was, so deception—it's safe to say—was her M.O.

"Yes, I remember him quite well!" she responded, turning bright red while smiling from ear to ear.

Rican shook his head, smiling at the thought of how Amanda fucked this White boy in the middle of the dance floor, and the crazy part was that everybody was truly oblivious as to what took place.

Tommy was this fly-ass, money-getting White boy that Rican met while doing a juvenile bid a few years back. Son was strictly about his paper.

NON-VIOLENT for sure, but a good dude.

"Keep this trip professional, A. Ride in and ride out because you have to get back . . . We have a lot of work to get out. Shit been on halt with all gunplay going on, so I'ma need y'all more than ever to get this worked out," he said sternly to show he was serious and took that way.

"Cool, I can do that. So what am I taking and am I supposed to collect anything?" Amanda replied, slightly disappointed but she fully understood her position.

"Two hundred fifty bricks, making ya collection twenty-five bands. On ya way back, drop that paper off at the spot out in Mays Landing and come straight back here to help them finish putting the rest of this shit together."

"Okay, so when do I leave?"

"Now!" Rican said while handing her a duffel bag filled with bricks of heroin. "And text me when you land," he added.

The rest of the girls were in class, but were about to get out within the next hour. Once they did, it was alright to work.

Rozay sat in the corner, staring out the window and thinking about everybody he had lost in such a short period of time. A piece of him wanted to leave the game behind and take his riches on the road, but the other part said, *Nah, fuck that.*

"Let's keep getting this fucking money and murda everything moving!"

Whatever the case may be though, his loyalty won't allow him to leave his family at war without him.

"We gotta get on this shit, G! All this sitting around shit . . . I gotta problem with that! These niggas are outta control and we here on some low shit?" Rozay expressed while still looking out the window, deep in thought.

Both men sat in silence, thinking about what was next to come.

"Let's ride. We out!" Rican broke the silence.

He grabbed a pen lying on the table and began to write instructions for the girls to follow once they arrived back home. The list involved them bagging up and dropping work off to a few suburban spots around the area.

"Where we goin'?" Rozay asked.

"You'll see!"

The men left the house, got in the car, and headed to the next destination, wherever that was.

Somewhere in Camden

Spizz met up with some old head cat named Splurge. Son had just come home from doing fifteen and was said to be a good nigga, real money-getting type. They met through one of the brodies from around the way. Apparently they were bunkies down state. Lil brah was still down, though they called him Weedie. Another non-violent type but truly about a dolla.

Weedie spoke highly of ol' head and put him in touch with Spizz on the money tip. With all the heat down the way, the team needed all the help they could get to move all of the work Spizz had.

"What up, youngin blood?" Splurge asked with the biggest smile on his face as if they had known each other for years.

Splurge was some short nigga, real slick-fly-type though. Still had his gold fronts and all, and Spizz was digging dude from the start. The way he carried himself was truly different. He reminded Spizz of somebody, but he couldn't quite place it.

"I'm as cool as one could get. I heard some good things about you, so I'm gone get straight to the point. How much work can handle?" Spizz said, reminding himself as well as the ol' head that this was not a meet-and-greet; it was for business purposes only.

"Whatever you lay on me, I can handle, but before we get into all of that, my man . . . Well, ya young boy Weedie spoke about a war on your hands? I'ma ol' school playa in this game right here and anything I can do to help . . . I'm here. This here is my block! I came home to this here and I have some ol' school shooters I came up with that loves nothing more than putting it down, so say the word and they there," Splurge spoke in his low raspy voice.

Spizz stood there, eyes locked with this possible new ally and thought about what was just. He liked the idea, but at the end of the day, it was Silence's call and not his, so for now he would deal with his side of things.

"I'll keep that in mind, but for now . . . I'ma start you off with two keys of that Afghan black tar. That'll be $150,000 and if you can handle more, it's there. I trust my lil bruh's judgment, so I trust you, but don't make me regret!"

Splurge smiled as he walked to the back of the car he drove to the meet and retrieved a duffel bag that contained $100,000. He walked back towards Spizz and handed him the bag.

"That's a hundred right there . . . I don't play about no paper, and the two will be good for this first go around. Let me get my spot popping and we can go from there. Remember . . . my team is always on go, youngin, and they don't miss."

"I'll have that work to you in a few hours," Spizz said as the men went their respected ways.

In the car, Spizz watched Splurge drive off as he thought to himself how it wouldn't be a bad idea to bring in outside support. He was definitely feeling the way that Splurge conducted himself, but *let's see if Silence feels the same way as he does.*

18

Deuce was Paco's cousin in Baltimore . . . a real savage-life type. He and Paco were close, so this beef—or, should I say, war—was on some personal shit for real. He and ten of his men that he brought with him where out in the Ville on the south side, where those boarder cats mostly operated. He used every resource available to him to destroy Silence and everyone around him.

One of the young boys directly under Paco, named Gabby, was the ear and direction that Deuce needed to get the upper hand on Silence.

Silence knew nothing about Deuce, but Deuce knew everything about him.

"What's our next move?" one of Deuces men asked as they loaded their weapons.

"It's on them. We made our move, so let's see what they do. You see, what they don't know is that we missed purposely. That was just to make our presence known, and now the game of war begins and we will kill them all," Deuce replied in a thick accent.

Gabby sat in a corner, rolling up. He thought about any useful information that could be used to flush Silence out.

"I know where Silence's daughter goes to school," Gabby said.

"No children!" Deuce said firmly. "Like I said, the next move is theirs . . . either they make it or I will make it for them, and this time we don't miss!"

Uptown in Atlantic City

Silence, his uncle Muhmit, and some old washed-up nigga named Louch sat in an alley on the side of an apartment building discussing future plans. Louch was a stone-cold crackhead, but in the same sense, he still had that killa instinct he possessed back in his prime.

Louch ran with the Salams throughout the '90s. They used to call him "Ghost" because that was exactly what he was: a fucking ghost. He got a dolla or two, but mainly murda was the lane, and that best suited him. This is why Silence had always looked up to and respected the old man, even now.

"So, what's up nephew? What's the urgency?" Muhmit asked, looking slightly confused as to what his nephew wanted with him and this old washed-up bum.

"Louch, I need you to relocate . . . I'm sure you hear all about this war going on and these new cats that have come into the mix I know nothing about—no patterns, no faces . . . nothing! Take a few of your people out to the south side of the Ville and start getting ya fix from them. I'll give you all the paper you need to go around as much as possible, but I need you to be on point: snap pictures, get license plate numbers, and locations on where these cats be at. They won't expect anything of you and your people. All you are to them is a bunch of crackheads. Get me everything you can about them and trust that I will take care of you and those around you," Silence said. He had turned around in his driver's seat to face Louch.

"Not a problem, youngin. I watched you grow up, and you and your crew have always been good to me, so I will get right on it," Louch replied.

"Cool. Listen out for the name Deuce; he is the target," Silence said as he pulled off a few hundred and passed it to Louch. "Be on point and make sure I get a play-by-play," Silence added.

Louch went on his way, leaving Silence and Muhmit alone.

Muhmit hasn't been in the streets for years, and he left them for a reason. He has also vowed never to return, no matter what. Muhmit had over twenty bodies under his belt but had never used a gun; in fact, he hated them because they were too loud. He'd rather get up close and personal—either slit your throat or stab you to death. He was also a master of kidnapping and torture. Right now, Silence needed his uncle and if his Muh agreed . . . the game is in trouble.

"Unc, I need you out of retirement!"

Downtown A.C.

Rican and Rozay sat up the block where Paco's sister lived, between Florida and Texas Ave. They learned of this location through Rozay's cousin who worked for the DMV. Rican remembered the license plate number on one of Paco's cars and recalled hearing that his car was in her name.

They sat in a black Ford F-250. It was kind of hard to imagine these two men squatting since it was two in the morning and the hard rain and wind kept most people off the streets anyway.

"So, are we going wait for her to come out or are we going in to get the bitch?" Rozay asked, growing impatient.

The plan was to kidnap the woman and hold her for ramson, but have Deuce meet for the drop because, right now, word is that he was running shit in place of Paco, so that was the head that needed to be cut off.

"We go in. When we rode past, I noticed an air conditioner on the first floor, right on the side of the crib. We take that out and climb in," Rican replied while passing the blunt back to Rozay.

"So, we're going to have to park on the side of the crib then," Rozay responded.

"Exactly."

Paco's sister, Zelda, was a schoolteacher who mainly dealt with special-needs students. A beautiful woman, mid-thirties, about 5'6", and built like something you'd see in one of those straight stunting magazines.

She lived on the nicer side of the city—a quiet little street with a tree line stretching up the block. Her spot was a two-story brick-style joint with the driveway on the side of the house, making it easier for the men to get in and get out unnoticed.

The house was dimly lit, so you could tell that whoever was there was asleep. She had a white Toyota Camry parked in the back under a makeshift shed, and three trash cans lined the side of her house. An air conditioner hung out of what appeared to be the living room window; it had a 2x4 holding it up. The blinds were slightly drawn, making it easy for Rican to look in to peep at the scenery.

There was a big brown leather sofa sitting directly in front of the window with the air conditioner, so it wouldn't really be a problem for the men to enter.

"We have to get something to stand on, so we can lift the air conditioner out," Rican said as he headed towards the back of the house in search of a chair or something.

Rozay stood slightly in front of the house, just enough that he couldn't be seen, to see if anyone was looking or driving up the block.

Rican returned with a green crate he found behind the makeshift shed.

"This should do!" he whispered. "Come on and help me get this shit out."

Rican worked to get the unit out of the window while Rozay held on to him and used his foot to keep the crate sturdy.

The 2x4 stopped the air conditioner from falling once the window was slid open. Rican reached in to slide the sides of the unit in. There were clamps on each side connecting it to the window.

Once the clamps were released, Rican stepped off the crate while keeping both hands on the unit.

Rozay removed the 2x4 and both men lowered the air conditioner to the ground. Before climbing in, he took one last peek around the front of the house to make sure everything was still clear. Satisfied with the scenery, the men proceeded to climb into the home.

They searched the first floor, making sure everything was clear. After seeing that it was, they continued to the stairs.

"Once we get up there, you take the left and I'll go right!" Rozay whispered.

Once upstairs, the men separated. At the top of the stairs was a bathroom a few feet to the left and a bedroom directly across from it. It looked like a child's room and it was empty. To the right was another room at the end of the hall. The door was closed, but you could see the TV light flickering at the bottom of the door.

At the door, both men locked eyes with each other. Rican tested it to see if it was locked, and it wasn't.

As he turned the knob gently and pushed the door open, Rozay peeked in and saw Zelda lying in bed with what appeared to be a man. It was hard to tell because of the blanket that was draped over their bodies.

Rozay stood at the foot of the bed with his gun drawn as Rican got into position and stood on the side where Zelda slept. He signaled to Rozay by counting with his fingers. When he got to three, they releases two muffled shots into the sleeping man's head, waking Zelda instantly.

Before she had a chance to scream, Rican covered her face with a rag that had been soaked in ammonia, knocking her right back out.

The two men hogtied the woman, put her into an oversized duffel bag, and carried her out to the back of the pickup truck they drove in. After placing her in the back, they covered her with the blue tarp that occupied most of the cab, and to the next destination they went.

CHAPTER

19

Silence and Spizz met up in one of the spots around the hood to discuss the situation with the cat, B-Boy. A few days before, he sent Silence everything he asked for regarding the next hit. Now, all that had to be done was to get his connections at the DMV to get addresses on both men, and then came the surveillance.

"Once I get everything I need, I will be out of town for a few days scoping this shit out," Silence said as he and Spizz watched the morning news while smoking their blunts.

"What you think about that shit, you know, the whole B-Boy thing?" asked Spizz.

Spizz never really met the cat, so he couldn't truly judge whether or not son seemed cool. He knew Silence was good at reading niggas, but in a sense Spizz also wanted to be sure that his bruh was good at all times. They were all each other had growing up, so looking out for one another was always a given.

"I'm still trying to read this nigga. Something is there and I'm going to figure this shit out because the situation doesn't make too much sense . . . All of those shooters that he is said to have and he needs me?" Silence replied between puffs of his weed.

"But I may be wrong, so I'm going to go and scope the scene; then we go from there. How's business, though?"

Spizz ignored the question for a second or two, still focused on the B-Boy thing.

"Work is moving, not how it should, but I'm getting to it. I linked up with some all head playa out in Camden. Weedie plugged him in.

He vouched, so for now, he good," Spizz replied. "He also offered help with this war," he added.

"Is that right?" Silence responded with a smirk.

As they were talking, Spizz caught a glimpse of the TV screen and became extremely quiet.

"Turn that up!" Spizz said as he focused in on the headline of the news.

Man found dead in the downtown area of the city, apparent kidnapping, the bottom of the screen read.

"Apparently someone climbed into the side of this home behind me and killed a man in his late thirties. It is said to be tied to a kidnapping of a local schoolteacher, Zelda Ortiz. Police have no suspects, and as you can see, if you look to the left and right, police and detectives are going house to house to see if anyone noticed any strange activity or if anyone even heard anything overnight here in this quiet city street," spoke the news anchorwoman.

Silence and Spizz looked at each other, noticing that it was Paco's sister that had been allegedly kidnapped.

"Have you spoken to either of them niggas?" Silence asked, slightly enraged by what he just saw on the news.

If it were his men, he wouldn't be that upset about the action. It would be the fact that they made a big move without his approval. That was extra heat they didn't need as a whole. Strategic, yeah, but Silence had a better way and now things will be harder to execute because of this extra heat.

"Nah. Last time I heard they were out in G-Way with Amanda and the girls, putting the work together," Spizz said as he pulled out his phone to call Rican.

Somewhere out in the sticks

Rican and Rozay had Zelda tied to a chair in the basement of this abandoned farmhouse in the next county over. They had used this spot quite a few times over the years. It was in a very secluded area and there wasn't another house nor property around for miles.

"Spizz just hit me. He said Silence needs to see us like now . . . we should have ran this shit by bruh first," Rican said.

They knew this action was an impulse move, but they couldn't not do anything at all.

"Yeah, you right, but fuck it—what's done is done, so let's just deal with bruh and move on," Rozay replied.

"I just texted him our location. He said they'd be here within the next hour, so sit tight," said Rican.

Out in the Ville

Deuce and his men were in a trap house next door to the spot that was fired-bombed a while back when Silence and his men executed most of the Dominican cartel—well, at least the ones in this area. He had just found out about his cousin being kidnapped and you could tell he was clearly not in the right state of mind to be leading.

He was a nut by nature, but in his eyes, women and children were off limits. Now those rules were out the window, especially since Silence crossed that line.

"Get his daughter," Deuce said through clenched teeth.

His men all looked at each other wondering who would carry out this task. I mean, it couldn't be done at the moment because it was the weekend and school was out.

"No one really knows where he lives, Deuce. He's cautious like that, and following him is next to impossible," Gabby said in a very low tone.

Deuce stood facing his men with a blank expression as he thought about his next move.

"So I take it that it's on us now?" he said to no one in particular.

"Gabby, do you know that location of their stash houses?" Deuce asked as a plan came together in his head.

"Yeah, I know of two; one is gated and can't be touched, but I know where the bitches be that live there and maybe we can snatch one of them up to get in. He also has one around their projects . . . We can forget about that one." Gabby replied.

"Get them bitches . . . NOW!"

Meanwhile, back at the ranch

Silence and Spizz had just arrived at the farmhouse where his men were keeping Deuce's cousin, Zelda. The men sat at the table in the kitchen in complete silence as Silence smoked his blunt and talked on the phone with Tish. He was telling her to not to leave the house unless he said otherwise and not to make any outside phone calls.

He couldn't risk anything happening to his wife and daughter.

"What the fuck was you lil niggas thinking?" he finally said, directing his full attention to Rican and Rozay. "Don't y'all know what type of heat this shit gone bring? We already got enough of that as it is!"

"I'm saying Si, I felt as though we had to make our move. Yeah, you running shit, but my paper is slowing up because of this war and not to mention all the niggas we lost to them bean-eating motherfuckas. I take full responsibility for this shit though, but this shit gotta end big bruh," Rozay said.

Silenced had a genuine love for these two men. Yeah, he was hot about the way they handled this, but he also knew that sometimes in this game you had to take things to drastic measures to get shit done.

"So what was the play?" Silence asked, wanting to hear about their elaborate plan.

The men looked at each other before Rican answered.

"We were going to call them niggas and tell them that if they wanted this bitch back to bring a half mil to a meet-up spot, but the catch was that the nigga Deuce had to bring it. Cut the head off, the body gone fall!" Rican answered.

Silence and Spizz locked eyes.

Spizz shrugged his shoulders, saying that it wasn't a bad idea.

"Do it!" said Silence.

Another issue needed to be discussed involving the distribution of the work that Spizz had been having to sit on. Yeah, work was moving but not the way that it should. It had been too much murder, so now Spizz had to figure out a way around, at least until this war was over.

"Rican, I'ma need you to reach out and get with Fresh. See what he's doing and if he can put some work back out in Sicklerville for us.

Let me know. We'll give him the bricks for ninety each, but he has to take no less that 500 of 'em," Spizz said.

"I'm on it. I got Amanda and the girls giving out work and collecting paper now, but even with that, we still sitting on about fifteen keys dope and a couple of coke. You know we had the bros out in Cumberland and Salem County, but they ain't with us no more, and with this war, we haven't had a chance to send nobody out there," said Rican.

Spizz thought for a moment about who he could trust to handle that territory Aido and Rico once controlled.

"Send Duke," he said. "I know he just came home, but shorty smart as shit and be money hungry, so let him know he has his shot: do not to blow it. And make sure them bitches is round-the-clock putting that work together, out of that fifteen, break down four more and the rest I'll wholesale. I gotta nigga out in Camden that be moving and he just called for five of them things, so we'll be good for the moment."

Silence sat listening to his team. This lane has never been his, but he always paid close attention as a means of making sure Spizz never made a mistake.

"Dig, y'all handle that situation with Deuce like now. The faster the better. I have some things to take care of O.T., so I'll be gone and out of touch for a few days, but be smart and get this clown out the way . . . Protect the family, and protect what's right," said Silence before the men went their separate ways.

20

Tish sat on the edge of her bed crying as she thought about the call she just received from Silence. He had never instructed her to do anything like this before and it worried her, not just for their child's sake, but for Silence's as well. Tish knew he could handle his own, but she just couldn't help thinking about what-ifs.

"Mommy, is daddy coming home tonight?" asked their daughter, Nazia, as she came in holding her favorite toy while rubbing her tired eyes.

Tish couldn't hide her tears. As much as she wanted to, she couldn't.

"Daddy is out working, baby, but I know he will be home as soon as he can. Just go back to bed," she replied.

"Can I sleep here with you?"

Tish couldn't help but smile. Her baby girl looked so much like her father.

"Of course, baby. Come on," said Tish with open arms as they both prepared to take it down for the night.

"Can we pray for daddy?" Nazia spoke in almost a whisper.

"Sure, baby."

Pistol Pete's Bar out in the Ville

Gabby and two of Deuce's men were at the pool table shooting a game and throwing back shots. No one had any idea they were there with the intention of kidnapping the two White girls over by the bar. Amanda and Jessica were totally oblivious to the fact that they were being watched by the men. In fact, they were too drunk to even bother to notice.

Gabby knew this was a spot the girls frequented often and figured what better way to get close to them than to catch them all out of their element.

Javier, one of Deuce's closest friends, were among the men—a real smooth type cat—you know, the Rico Suave type . . . The plan was for him to go over and party with the women to get them to open up and possibly take them home with them.

As Javier walked over to the women, he locked ayes with Jessica and all that she could do was smile. Jessica was a natural blonde, not the dippy type but real down to earth, a little giddy but head strong. She would remind you a lot of Alyssa Milano, to get a better visual.

As he approached, she said, "Hello handsome!" She slurred slightly as she rubbed her hand over his chest.

Javier knew he had her where she needed to be and he thought this task wouldn't be so hard after all.

Gabby and Tito watched from a distance, admiring their companion's flirtatious tactics. If it had been up to Gabby, they would have just thrown the bitches in the trunk and kept it pushing. But that wouldn't have flown because of the gated community where they lived; the men needed them to get in.

"Hey, mami. I'm Javier . . . and you are?" he asked as he took her right hand in his and kissed it.

"Perfect gentlemen, huh? Well, my name is Jessica and this is my best friend, Amanda," replied the unsuspecting victim.

"Well, it's a pleasure to meet you both. Can I get you two anything to drink?" asked Javier, thinking the drunker, the better.

"No, thank you. We've had enough!" Amanda jumped in, giving him the hint that she wanted nothing to do with him or what he had to offer.

"Don't mind her. She's evil," Jessica said. She made a face and poked Amanda on the shoulder in jokingly. "A double shot, if Ciroc will be just fine," she added.

The men didn't know these women were up to a trick of their own. You see, Amanda recognized Gabby from the moment he walked in.

She remembered riding with Rican one day and spotting him at light before the whole beef popped off. She recalled him telling her who he was and who he ran with.

Amanda was well aware of the war that was going on, so while Javier was spitting his weak-ass game, she was texting Rican to let him know what was going on. She knew the game well enough to know these men had a motive, but they would soon realize they were not the typical White girls, and that they had a motive of their own.

Somewhere in Hoboken, N.J.

Silence was at his second stop. Before arriving in Hoboken, he made a pit stop in Elizabeth to scope out the cat named Maurice, who was also part of the contract placed by B-Boy.

Maurice's spot seemed pretty typical and Silence had no problems at all getting the full rundown on him from one of his neighbors. He lived in a predominately Hispanic neighborhood and everybody that Silence spoke to seemed not to be very fond of the dude, so no questions were raised when Silence came around. If they did question him, he'd use the cousin-from-out-of-state line; since he had Maryland tags on the Buick Regal he drove, it would have been an easy story to sell.

Silence sat a few houses away from the address he had on his other target. They called him Sport, but his name was Rondell Goodin. He lived on a dead-end street, which seemed like a nice spot to lie low—very quiet, a secluded block covered with trees all up and down the sidewalks. This would make it easier for Silence make a move on his soon-to-be victims.

He was only there for an hour before he saw his target pulling out of the driveway in a white Lexus GS 450. As soon as he rode past, Silence started his rental and followed a few car lengths behind.

His plan was to follow him for a few days to learn his day-to-day activities: what time he got home at night, what he did for a living, who he dealt with, and how cautious he was when doing whatever it was that he was into.

Silence knew Sport had a wife and two kids—a teenage boy and a little girl. The wife was always home; she didn't work. She was more so the stay-at-home type and, from what Silence learned, dude keeps it like that for security reasons . . . You know, to keep the paper safe. Now let's just see how that works out for him.

Silence has already collected the $100,000 up front, so with another $100 for Maurice's bitch and her brother that stays with him, along with another $150 for the nigga Sport's family . . . that's $350,000 off B-Boy. Silence just may like this nigga after all, or so he thought.

Back at the bar

"Come on, ladies. How would you like to chill with me and my friend over there?" Javier asked, in hopes they would take the bait.

Amanda continued to stall for time because Rican was out Philly when she hit him and he told her he'd be there in about an hour. It had only been half an hour.

"How about we have a few more drinks first," Jessica suggested.

"Aight, cool, but let me introduce you fine ladies to my boys!" he slurred over the semi-loud music as he waved for Gabby and Tito to come over.

Amanda continued texting Rican, giving him a play-by-play of what was taking place. He and told her that once they got back in the area, they'd get the bikes and be right there; but stressed for them to play along and keep them there until she received his text.

"Ladies, this is Gabby, and this here is my main man, Tito. He doesn't speak much English but understands it clearly," Javier said as his men walked up to where they were sitting at the edge of the bar.

Back in Hoboken

Silence watched as Sport made countless drops all around the city. He was impressed by how he conducted his business, but less impressed by how he was not aware of his surroundings.

"This nigga is an easy target, especially for a stickup kid," Silence said out loud to himself.

The last stop Sport made for the day got Silence more curious than ever. Throughout the day, every day, every drop this nigga made, he either carried a bag in or carried one out. But this stop was on the side of a library. Sport parked in the front, but walked to the side and went into the side door. He looked around as if he didn't want to be seen, and that was strange, especially since that was the first time he was on point all day.

Silence waited patiently across the street for his target to make his way back out.

"Something is up with this nigga," he thought to himself.

Back at the bar

Rican had just texted Amanda to let her know he would be there within the next five minutes so. He gave her instructions that when she heard the bikes, to go back in as if they forgot something. The men were having a good ol' time, or so they thought, and Gabby swore that their plan was coming together just fine.

"Are you guys ready to get out of here or what?" Amanda asked while still looking at her phone.

"Yeah, let's roll!" Javier replied, ready to get down to the real business at hand.

As the group began exiting the bar, Amanda heard the sounds of street bikes from a distance and knew exactly what was next.

"Oh, shoot. Y'all go ahead and wait out front for us. I forgot my wallet at the bar."

"Aight, cool," said the men as they exited the bar.

The men stepped out into the parking lot and began to walk towards their car. Before they made it halfway there, a dozen shots were let off from what sounded like an assault rifle. The first shot ripped through Gabby's head, hitting Tito in the neck as Javier tried ducking behind a nearby parked car.

Rozay got off his bike and hit Tito three times in his head, finishing him off, while Rican continue to spray the car Javier was seen running behind. Sirens began to approach, so Rican was the first to pull away from the bar, speeding up the pike, but not before Rozay crept around the car, hitting Javier with the rest of his clip.

CHAPTER

21

Spizz, Rican, and Rozay were down in the basement at the farmhouse with their victim, who was still tied to a chair. Zelda had not eaten in days. It wasn't because she refused to eat; it was the fact that the men hadn't taken the time out to feed this woman. Yeah, they gave her water daily, but I guess starvation was a part of their torture.

The men were there discussing the event from the angle that Deuce was trying to play when Rican got the call from Amanda saying these men were at the bar and that one just approached them.

The basement was dark and dim, and the only light was from the flashlight Rozay was holding up. There was a foul stench of mold, rust, piss, and bowel movements that made it difficult for the men to breathe; not to mention water was dripping from the upper level from a rain the night before.

"So Deuce sent those niggas last night to get at my bitches?" Spizz asked after getting informed of the events from the night before."

Spizz handpicked these ladies personally and they were extremely loyal to the cause, especially since he paid all of their tuition and, on top of that, made sure they never wanted for anything. All he ever asked for was loyalty—no pussy, just loyalty!

"Yeah, that's how shit was looking, but the girls were on it; they hit me as they peeped the game. I'm guessing they were going to hit that spot and use the work that was there as some kind of leverage to get shorty back," Rozay replied.

Spizz stood there for a moment, thinking of their next move. Knowing what Silence would do, he made the decision to conduct the situation similarly.

"Cut her hands off and have them delivered to Deuce personally. Let him know he has twenty hours to get us a half mil and for him to meet up and come alone. We'll text him the location. Anything past the mark, and she dies," Spizz said before exiting the property.

Spizz usually didn't handle that side of the business—you know, the murder game—but it got more personal to him once Deuce attempted to interfere with his money. The war had already slowed up the process, but now he wanted to take from him. Nah, you don't do shit like that.

"That would be my pleasure!" Rican smiled as he walked to the corner of the basement and grabbed a rusted-out back saw.

G-way

Silence made it back to the city after about a week on the road. He had everything he needed to execute his plan. All he had to do now was take care of his own personal problem—and he had another plan for that.

Silence sat in the living area of the condo where Amanda and the girls lived as he watched them go to work bagging up Spizz's product. Amanda, Jessica, and Karen were at the kitchen table wearing nothing but aprons, latex gloves, and face masks. They chopped up dope while Lynn sat in the middle of the living room floor a few feet from Silence counting money.

Silence truly admired Lynn, not just because she was beautiful but also because she was quiet . . . almost like scary quiet. All she did most of the time was smile, but you can tell there was something evil in those eyes. It probably stemmed from being molested by her stepfather growing up, but whatever it was, the evil was there.

Lynn was a little taller than the rest of girls. She stood at 5'10", real thick for a White girl, and rocked a little pixie cut dyed black . . . Definitely something you can pull up with and stop time for sure. Shorty could have easily been a model of something.

"Lynn, let me talk to you for minute or two," said Silence, still studying her movements.

Lynn was the only one of the girls who wasn't intimidated by him; in fact, she had always had a little crush on Silence but kept that to herself.

As she finished counting the last stack she was working on, she wrapped a rubber band around it before going over and sitting on the edge of the table directly in front of Silence.

"Yes," she answered in a low but sensual and seductive voice.

Silence smiled, seeing the lust in her eyes but kept things professional.

"How do you feel about murder?" he asked, getting straight to the point.

As soon as he asked the question, Lynn crossed her legs and began biting down on her lip while rubbing her thighs. It was unintentional; that was just her reaction.

"Lynn!" Silence said, slightly confused as he tapped her on her leg.

Snapping back out of it, she apologized and covered her face out of embarrassment and turned beet-red. Silence smiled again.

"I guess that answers my question," he said to her as he pulled her hands away from her face, letting her know that it was cool to be turned on by violence.

"So, would you ever be up to murder someone?" he asked with a stern look on his face.

He knew there wasn't anything Lynn wouldn't do for him, especially since he was the one who murdered her stepfather for her when she confided in him about the things he made her do to him.

"Well, I fantasize about it a lot. You know, me killing somebody. I think about different ways of doing it. I would never want to use a gun, though, because those are too loud," she responded as she drifted into her own personal thoughts. "Why do you ask?" she added, snapping back into reality.

They sat there for a minute eyes and looked into each other's before he smiled and replied, "You work with me now!"

Southside

Louch lingered among a bunch of other friends while copping his fix. As he was waiting in line, he overheard a young kid name Cholo speaking about Deuce and how he was on his way around here and something about a package. He was given specific instructions to text Silence if there were ever any sign of Deuce.

Deuce was very cautious not be out in the open because of past bad experiences and he often made it a point to meet in closed-in and secluded areas.

"Aye, youngin, let me get three," Louch said while handing his folded-up money over to the young hustler.

As he was walking away, he overheard the young boy Cholo yelling to another youngin that Deuce was rolling up at the other end of the block.

Hearing this, Louch texted Silence and informed him of what was going on. He also texted how many people were out there and the kinds of cars he saw that lined the block.

—m—

Deuce parked his black Camaro on the side of one of the trap houses. He stepped out onto the front to catch a glimpse of who was out.

He carried a box that was delivered to the trap house by a UPS driver via certified mail earlier that day. Inside were the hands of his cousin Zelda with a note demanding a half mil.

Deuce was enraged and wanted nothing more than to murder anything moving, but first he had to think of his next move and how he'd get this kidnapping thing out of the way without being killed.

"Get the money!" he said to Cholo through clenched teeth.

Cholo didn't budge. He stood there with his head down, contemplating how he'd bring up the murders of Gabby and the other men.

He and Gabby grew up together. He understood the money thing for the kidnapping, but he also wanted revenge for his friend.

"What about what them motherfuckas did to our people? Are we supposed to just let that shit ride?" Cholo finally spoke up.

Deuce was well aware of his plan going sideways. He hated that his enemy was a few steps ahead of him, but getting his cousin back was more important than the men he lost, so for now that would be on the back burner.

"We'll get to that later, but for now we have to get Zelda back. I have until 4 p.m. tomorrow evening and they want me to come alone. I gotta figure out a plan because I know that I will be walking into my death," replied Deuce, feeling slightly defeated.

The men were unaware of the trouble that crept around the corner. Muhmit drove his motorcycle up the block with one target in mind . . . Deuce.

As Muhmit rode up, he pulled out a .40-caliber Desert Eagle with an extended clip.

Deuce and Cholo were still in deep conversation and the rest of his men were preoccupied by the car full of women that Silence sent there a few minutes before Muhmit arrived.

As Muhmit got closer, he rang off the first shot, hitting Cholo in the face. The second shot pierced Deuce's shoulder, sending him flying to the side of the trash can a few feet behind.

Deuce's men realized what was going on and started shooting at Muhmit, who has sped off, swerving back and forth to keep them off their aim.

Cholo lay there dead as Deuce finally stood up with his gun drawn looking in the direction where the gun man had fled.

"What the fuck, none of you idiots saw this guy coming? He was on a fucking bike; how can you not hear that?" he said as he approached the kid closest to him and shot him in the head.

The rest of the men were speechless. They knew how crazy this cat was, but to kill one of his own . . . that made these men fear him even more.

Sirens could be heard in the distance, so the men started getting into their cars and began pulling out in the opposite direction of the police.

"Fix this!" he yelled to one of his men as he pulled off in his Camaro, holding his shoulder.

CHAPTER

22

The block was swarming with fiends as they all came for their early morning. Spizz and his team had the best dope in the city, and fiends from all walks of life could be seen in and out of their project. From hustlers and lawyers to the neighborhood scum bags, everybody could get caught leaving this three-block radius.

Rozay sat on the stoop, watching the morning traffic as he spoke on the phone with one of his little hood bitches.

"I told you last night that I wouldn't be there when you woke up, so what the fuck is the problem?" he said into the phone receiver.

Rican was O.T. with Duke, showing him around so he can go out there on his own and set up shop in place of the team's fallen soldiers, leaving Rozay alone to make sure the hood ran the way it should.

"Aye, big brah . . . we down to the last seventy joints and they ain't gone last through the next hour!" one of the youngins said as he walked up, passing Rozay the blunt he was smoking.

"Shit shaking out this bitch, huh?" he replied.

This was a shock because these past few weeks, shit had been moving slow because of all the shooting that had been taking place, but now that things were getting back to the way they were, more work needed to be put back into the hood.

"I'll have some more shit dropped off within the next hour, so we'll be good." he assured the youngin.

He pulled his phone back out to text Amanda or one of the girls to drop off more dope.

Somewhere in Philly

It was training day for Lynn, who Silence had taken under his wing. He had a plan for this suburban White and he'd do everything he could to turn her into the killer he needed her to be.

Silence knew the situation he'd possibly face in the future would need a woman such as Lynn. She was well-educated, had a very innocent look, and not to mention she was White—and that was the bonus.

"You see that guy standing over by the coffee shop wearing the blue blazer?" he asked as they were parked across the street in Lynn's white Jaguar.

"Yes, I see him," Lynn replied.

She sat there as if that was something she did on a regular basis—you know, stake out a potential victim. No worry on the face, no sign of being nervous . . . in fact, she was as just as calm as Silence, if not calmer.

The man Silence brought Lynn to kill was one of the jewelers the team often used and the one Silence used to design Tish's engagement ring.

This man went by Chase and had a partner named Jason, the man who had sent Silence. He knew this job required outside help because Chase traveled with an entourage and two bodyguards.

Chase and Jason were not the typical town jewelers. They designed jewelry for all of the heavy hittas as well as a few celebrities from the Philly area. Apparently Chase had been scheming money from the business and had plans of branching off to do his own thing and take most of their clientele with him. That was how this hit came into place.

Getting to Chase was a difficult task. Not that he couldn't get it done; he just had too much on his plate at the moment and he knew using a woman of Lynn's caliber would get the job done faster.

Now all he needed was to mold Lynn into killer he knew she could be.

"He is your target . . . every morning around, 7:30, he goes into that coffee shop right there, and stays for about an hour before leaving. I noticed the type of women he hits on and you fit the bill perfectly," Silence said as they both watched the man getting into the back seat of a $550 Benz. "You're gonna have to play the coffee shop for a few days.

127

You know, sit in there with your laptop and act busy, which shouldn't be hard being that you may already have school work that needs to be done."

Lynn sat there studying the area as she listened closely to Silence. She was ready and looked forward to what was next to come. She vowed to herself to give this job her all because she did not want to let Silence down, especially since he was the one who got revenge for her regarding her creep of a stepfather.

"Then what?" she asked.

"You have to get him alone, get him comfortable enough to trust you that he'd be willing to go out with just you and him. Everywhere he takes you, be on the lookout for anybody that may be with him. When it comes to hotels, pay attention to security, look for cameras, and try wearing something that can easily make identifying you hard to figure out . . . glasses, hats, anything you can get away with without causing suspicion," Silence said, looking her dead in the eye to make sure she was paying close attention, which she was.

"Are you ready for this?" he asked.

"I was made to be this!" she replied as she thought about the torture she went through growing up.

"Good, because I really need you on this and I promise when this is done you'll have a big payday," Silence said.

Lynn turned away from Silence and gazed out of the window for a few minutes before speaking again. For her, this wasn't about the money and it wasn't just for the loyalty she felt she owed Silence for what he did . . . she wanted to do this for herself.

Lynn had a lot of pent-up anger in her. Over the years, she has dealt with this by shutting people out of her life, including her mother. She couldn't get close to a man because she felt as though she couldn't trust any of them, but with Silence, it felt different. Now she was at a point in her life where she no longer could hold in this pain; it was time to make others suffer the way she did all her life. And what better way to do it than murder?

"I'm not doing this for money, Si. I'm doing this because I want to. It's time for me to vent and, through murder, that is what I will do. I promise not to let you down because I do feel as though I owe you everything—because you gave me my freedom back when you killed my stepfather and that debt can never be repaid. Just tell me what to do, when to do it, and to whom I am doing it to, and I will get it done," Lynn replied with tears in her eyes, not from hurt but from sincerity.

Silence took her hand in his as he thought to himself about the future of this woman in front of him. He knew what he saw in her was real and also knew she had genuine loyalty for him and his team, but he wasn't prepared for the killer he was about to create.

"You start tomorrow!" he responded with a devious smile while looking forward to see how'd she do with her very first mission.

Back around the way

The block continued to flow with traffic and things were looking good for business's sake. Amanda had just dropped off 250 bricks of dope, so product was plentiful. Spizz was on his way around the hood to check on things and to pick up the paper that was waiting for him.

"Yo . . . you seen Champ?" Rozay yelled across the playground to his young boy, Danny.

Danny ran the trap house in the hood. Spizz handpicked him personally to keep order when he, Rican, and Rozay couldn't be around.

Danny was a natural-born hustler. Since a youngin, all he knew was to trap and he had never been one to play about any type of paper. That's why Spizz and the rest of the family loved 'em.

"He went to the corner store to get some wraps!" he said as he walked up to the car waiting for him.

"I'll be back in a minute. I gotta grab some shit for my daughter . . . my nut-ass B.M. keep blowing my shit up," Danny said as he got into the car.

Spizz had just hit the corner in a red Corvette when a gray Escalade pulled up at the other end of the block.

As both cars reached the middle of the street, all four doors of the SUV flew open and four masked men jumped out, spraying AK 47s in Rozay's direction. The first few shots hit the door behind Rozay and, as they continued firing off, Spizz hit the driver in the head with a shot from his .357 automatic.

At the same time, Rozay fired back, hitting the second gunman in the left leg before getting hit himself twice in the torso, sending him flying into the porch steps.

Spizz continued firing while taking shots as the passenger ran around to the driver side and jumped in. He and other two passengers sped past Spizz, leaving their dead driver behind.

Sirens were heard in the distance and one of the youngins ran up, taking Spizz's gun from him and telling him to get the fuck out of the Dodge.

Rozay lay there holding his stomach while gasping for air. Neighbors came out with towels and water to help aid him until an ambulance came. A friend close by took the gun that was still in his hand and got rid of it before the police and the ambulance arrived.

"Hold on, you'll be alright. Just fight," the elderly woman said into his ear.

CHAPTER

23

There were at least a hundred people gathered outside the hospital awaiting for a report on Rozay's condition. Silence, Spizz, Rican, and a few of the youngins were sitting in the hospital lobby discussing what had just occurred and how they were going to move forward with this war.

The police were also waiting around to question Rozay as to what took place—and not just with him, but also the other dead man on the scene. It's doubtful charges would be brought up due to the lack of police cooperation, so charging him or even considering doing so would be next to impossible.

The last these men heard, a doctor came to tell them Rozay was still in surgery and that it was extremely hard to tell at the moment whether or not he would pull through.

Rican was taking this the hardest of all of the men. He and Rozay had the same relationship as Silence and Spizz—they were childhood friends. He sat quietly with tears in his eyes, totally ignoring the conversations that were going on around him. The only thought that was going through his mind was to kill Deuce.

What these men didn't know was that Deuce did not order this hit. He was smarter than that, especially since they still had his cousin held hostage.

This act was carried out by Deuce's second-in-command, a cat they called Fuego. You see, Fuego was a non-thinking type of nigga. He figured the hit would be a better step in a different direction, but lo and behold, he just made things worse—not just for him, but for Deuce and his family as well.

"I can't believe this nigga . . . How the fuck he gone do some shit like this when we the ones holding the ace?" Spizz said to no one in particular.

"Kill Zelda!" Silence said, looking directly at Rican. "Cut the bitch's head off and have it dropped off in the middle of their block. From this point on, we move full force and we hit houses, blocks, and anybody you see in association with them cats . . . you kill. And find Deuce!" he continued before getting up and pulling Spizz to the side.

A lot had to be discussed about what to do regarding B-Boy as well.

"Before we get down to business, I wanted to let you know that I have Lynn on a job. She'll be working under me now, so you might not be seeing much of her," said Silence.

"I'm cool with that. The other three can handle things without her," he assured Silence as his mind raced about his next payday when Silence fulfills his next hit.

"These papi cats are really starting to get on my fucking nerves," Silence said as he flipped through his phone in search of B-Boy's number.

"I feel you, brah, but what are we going to do about them niggas?" replied Spizz.

It's known that the war and the murder game were not really his lane; he was hoping Silence had a plan to end this shit, so that he can put all of his focus back on getting money.

"I'm working on getting more info on where Deuce lays his head and I have constant surveillance on his block, so every time he pops his head up around there, I'll know and shooters will always be on standby," he answered.

The main shooter he was referring to was his Uncle Muhmit. It was hard getting him to come out of his slump, but Silence got it done.

Muhmit is the one who taught Silence everything he needed to know about the murder game. In his prime, even up until a few years ago, Muhmit still did his own thing in the game, but his lane was more on home invasions than anything. He fell out of the loop when his partner in crime was killed by the police after doing a robbery in the uptown area in the city. Muhmit was supposed to be there with him but decided not to do the job, forcing his friend to take some other cat who didn't quite know what he was doing.

Long story short, things went south and his man wound up dead. Until this day, he blames himself because he figured if he had been there, none of what happened would have gone down and his man would still be there. Ever since, he vowed to leave the streets alone . . . up until now.

Silence was in the middle of texting B-Boy to let him know things would be in motion soon when a gray Dodge Magnum pulled up in front of the hospital where they were standing. A tall slightly older Dominican woman got out of the passenger seat and walked up to them asking where she could find Silence.

"Who's asking?" Spizz asked, stepping closer to the woman.

The woman sensed the hostility, so she put her hands in the air in a suggestive manner to ensure she was indeed harmless and explained she was only the messenger.

"I'm Silence," he said while moving Spizz to the side, so that he's facing the woman.

The woman put her head down as tears began to fill her eyes. Before one could fall, she spoke. "I am Zelda's aunt. I hear you were the one who killed my sister, my nephew, and now you have my niece. My name is Gloria and I am here begging you to release Zelda. My son Deuce has sent me here. He has explained what happened to your friend and asked me to come to talk to you. He says he had nothing to do with the hit and said he would take care of all responsible parties. He asked for you not to take this situation out on Zelda . . . I'm also begging you. I understand that it is money that you want, well, I will deliver the money personally, but please just let my niece go," the woman begged. "You do not have to worry about me going to the police. That is a no-no in our family!" she assured the men.

Silence stood there studying the woman, looking for any sign of dishonestly or mischief before speaking again. "Tell him I will be in touch," he said while signaling to Spizz that the conversation was over and they were going back inside.

The woman stood there watching them walk away from her. The longer she stood there, the more her anger grew. And as her anger grew more, she couldn't help but break down as she got back into her car and peeled out of the hospital parking lot.

Back inside the waiting area, Silence and Spizz stood off to the corner away from everybody to discuss the hits that would be taking place within the next few weeks.

"I went out the way, and once I get everything in order we will be O.T. for a few days taking care of business," he said to Spizz while looking around to be sure no one could over hear their conversation. "Both spots look pretty simple. I have escape routes in play. I'm waiting for the cars we will use to go out the way, and I'm sure you will make out with at least one of them. I followed the cat around in Hoboken for a few days and son seems as though he's getting to a bag, so there that go," he continued.

"So when exactly are we going to do this?" Spizz asked looking forward to seeing his next payday.

It wasn't like Spizz was hurting for cash; he was just greedy when it came to money and as stated before, he saw no point in leaving all that paper in each victim's crib for the police to just confiscate.

"I'll keep you posted on that, but soon. Right now we have to get this situation with this war in check. The shit is giving me a fucking headache," Silence replied.

"Word, who you telling? My flip time slowed up because of this shit, but what we gone do and how we gone hit?" asked Spizz.

Silence knew his team was more frustrated with this beef shit than he was and, for their sake, he'd end this one way or another.

As they walked back over to where Rican was sitting, they bumped into a young woman claiming to be pregnant by Rozay. She wanted to know what the status was with her child's father. The problem with that was, nobody—including Rican—knew who this woman was or had ever seen her before.

Rozay and Rican had no secrets, and this woman appeared to be at least seven months pregnant. Something didn't add up. Either Rozay was hiding the bitch or she was put up to this.

"Can I see him?" the woman asked with tears in her eyes.

The men looked at each other, knowing something was off, but played along anyway.

"Nah, shorty. Nobody can see 'em yet. He's still in surgery. I mean, if you want to wait around, you can sit with us until we hear something," Spizz said while studying her reaction.

"No, I have to get to work, but I will check back after my shift. Don't tell him I came by because I want to surprise him!" she responded with a slight smile.

"What's ya name, again?" Rican asked through clenched teeth.

He knew one of them niggas sent this bitch to finish his man and it was hard for him to contain it.

Silence grabbed his shoulder and told him to relax as he escorted the woman to the exit and out to her car.

The parking lot was still filled with concerned faces, all of which were from their projects. As Silence passed through the crowd, he leaned into one of the youngins from around the way and told him to follow this woman; if she went anywhere near the direction of them boarder cats, he was to kill her.

Once back at the hospital, the men continued their plan to move forward. It was decided that they would kill Zelda and a team would be sent out to their projects to execute anyone that was out.

What these men didn't know was that Deuce's right-hand man, Fuego, was the one calling these shots. You see, Fuego felt as though Deuce was getting soft and decided to take action on his own . . . but will it backfire?

"Roger Lewis," the doctor said as he came into the lobby reading his chart looking for anybody that was there for Rozay.

"Yeah, that's my brother!" Rican replied, getting up walking towards the doctor.

"Your brother will be okay. We have completed the surgery and it may take a while for him to recover, so we will keep him for a few more weeks. He has slight nerve damage on the left side of his body, but he'll be fine. A little physical therapy, and he'll be on his way," the doctor said.

"Can we see him?" asked Rican, relieved his friend would live.

"Not before we do!" a homicide detective said as he walked up, staring Rican down.

CHAPTER

24

Deuce, Fuego, and one of Fuego's hittas, a young kid who went by Sleep, all sat at the kitchen table at a friend's spot in their hood.

They were discussing what took place with Rozay the day before. Deuce wanted to know whose idea it was to go and do something too stupid because it put his cousin in more danger than what she was already in.

"Nobody moves unless I give you the go . . . What the fuck don't you fools understand about that!" said Deuce as he got up from the table and began pacing back and forth across the kitchen floor.

Fuego and Sleep just looked at each other, shaking their heads in unison. In their minds, Deuce was getting soft and theory and pushed him out of the way.

"Check. I understand the whole cousin situation—believe me, I do—but these niggas are playing a different ball game and we have to let shit be known that we all in just as they are. They not gone killing shorty because she is leverage as a means of getting you. Speaking of which . . . what are you doing about that?" Fuego asked. He folded his arms, waiting to hear his friend's bright idea.

Deuce hadn't quite figured that part out yet because he knew he would have walked right into a trap and wouldn't have made it out, but he also knew it was something that had to be done.

"I gotta bring 'em the money!" he responded, slightly defeated.

As the men continued their conversation, a motorcycle could be heard swerving up the block, followed by a few shots.

"See what I mean . . . They don't respect us!" Fuego said as they all ran to the front of the house, guns drawn.

Outside, several of Deuce's men were standing around a small duffel bag that was lying next to the curb. None of them wanted to get too close, not knowing if there was some sort of explosive device inside.

"What the fuck just happened?" asked Deuce as he walked up to the men surrounding the small duffel.

"Some cat on a bike just rode past and threw this bag. I let off a few shots trying to hit the dude, but I missed," replied one of the youngins.

"Open the bag!" Deuce sternly said still clutching his weapon.

Sleep walked over and picked up the bag. Blood started to drip from the bottom. As he opened it, he saw what was inside, so he calmly handed it to Deuce, letting him know it was for him.

"It's Zelda!"

Deuce looked in the bag and saw his cousin's head with the eyes cut out, and "war" carved into her forehead.

G-way

Lynn stood in the middle of the living room floor completely naked, dancing seductively for Silence. She was excited because of the hit. Everything went well and she knew Silence would be extremely proud of her. Killing the jeweler was not hard for Lynn at all; in fact, she kind of enjoyed it.

Lynn met the man at the coffee shop just as Silence said and, in a matter of days, they were alone in a room just off the highway. Lynn seduced the man into complete bliss and she even went as far as having an orgasm as she slit the jeweler's throat.

"Are you proud of me, Si?" she said while gyrating her hip and looking Silence dead in his eye.

Silence sat there smiling at his new protégé. Yeah, Lynn was sexy as hell, but he had no intentions of fucking her at all. He just enjoyed a good show every now and then. His intentions were to mold Lynn into the perfect assassin. He didn't know it then, but he'd need her more than he knew in the near future.

"Indeed, I am. And I will need you again very soon, but remember to keep this part of your life between us. Killers move quietly. Nobody should know of your crime but you and your victim, and always cover your tracks. Do your homework and remain patient," Silence replied as he continued to enjoy the show Lynn was putting on.

"Anything for you Si. Anything . . . Point them out and I will put them under. I never knew how sexy murder was and how much it would truly turn me on," said Lynn as she lay in the middle of the floor. She began to play with her pussy while still staring into Silence's eyes.

He sat there, still smiling and thinking to himself how interesting this woman in front of him truly was.

"That's good to know because I have another job for you," he responded.

Back at the hospital

After personally delivering Zelda's head to Deuce's block, Rican made his way back to the hospital to be with his friend. Rozay was doing a lot better. When Rican arrived, they had him downstairs with the physical therapist, working on his walk.

Usually it would have taken someone a lot longer getting to this point, but Rozay was a fighter and rage fueled his desire to get the show back on the road.

Rican found the room where his friend was and stood in the doorway. He watched as the nurse and therapist both stood on each side of Rozay as he walked on a treadmill to regain his strength, not just in his legs but his overall mental strength.

The bullets from the assault rifle tore through his torso and out of his back, missing by inches any main arteries, but the down side was the shit back he had to carry around for the next few months during the healing process.

"You're doing good, Mr. Howard, but you have to push a little harder if you want to be out of here within the next week. I can't clear you unless you can walk down this hall with no assistance," the therapist said while pointing at the doorway where Rican was standing.

"Yeah, playboy, you gotta push!" Rican said with a smile as he walked up to where the group was.

"How long you been standing there?" asked Rozay between deep breaths.

"Long enough to hear ya bitch ass grunting and moaning and shit," Rican replied while laughing and giving his boy a pound.

"Now, now . . . Give him a chance; he is trying," the nurse said with a smile.

"Excuse me, can y'all give us a few minutes? I have to holla at him about some family business," Rican kindly asked the nurses.

The therapist cut off the machine and slid a wheelchair close enough so Rozay could sit down without a problem.

"Okay, but we'll be back in ten minutes, Mr. Howard. You will not escape this session, not like yesterday," the nurse joked.

Once they were alone, Rican filled him in about Zelda and the plans he had as far as moving forward with this war.

"What happened with homicide?" Rican asked before he continued with their plans.

"I told them I had my back turned and the next thing I knew, I was hit. They asked about the other dead nigga and I told 'em, '. . . like I said, my back was turned and the next thing I knew, I was hit . . .' I don't know shit and ain't seen shit," Rozay replied.

There was nothing much they could do as far questioning Rozay, especially since he told 'em the next time they wanted to talk to make sure his lawyer was present.

"Word. I don't see them really pushing, I mean, they know, but they don't know . . . but fuck 'em. I talked to Silence and him and Spizz will be taking care of something O.T. within the next week. Not sure exactly when, but he said he's trying to tie things up with Deuce before they roll out. I say we just go out there and start doing the same cowboy shit they been doing to us," Rican replied.

"Yeah, I'm on that same wave, kid. I mean, look at me . . . They gotta a real nigga all out of commission and shit. At least when we come through, we kill. These niggas are shooting scared and that's the worst kind of rapid fire, so we gotta get at these niggas for real. Remember the firing-bombing shit?" asked Rozay. "I say we hit 'em the same, but all they spots. I'm not trying to miss none of them bean-eating ass goyas. They all gotta go, my nigga," he continued.

These men knew things were about to get a lot worse, and not just for them but for Deuce and his crew as well.

This war has come with way more heat than what they expected, and since the local authorities were unable to solve any of the homicides, they brought in the Feds for help.

"I feel you, kid. Shit definitely about to get thick, so we gotta act before them niggas do. Deuce is probably going wild over that Zelda shit," Rican replied.

"Whose idea was that? I mean, I know the plan was to use her to get to Deuce, but what leverage do we have now?" asked Rozay.

"Believe it or not, he was the one who said to cut the bitch's head off," Rican responded. "The plan now is to kill everybody. He put no limits on everybody; once he saw you all laid up and not knowing what was going to be, brah said all things are a go."

Rozay left feeling good, knowing the man he looked up to would go to hell and back for him like this. I mean, he already knew the love he had for him and Rican, but Silence going to the extreme for them told another story. And once he has recovered, he'd make certain that time never was or will ever be wasted.

"So what now?" Rozay asked again.

"You just get better. In the meantime . . . we kill!" replied Rican as the therapist and nurse made their way back into the room.

CHAPTER

25

"So what's the plan?" Spizz asked Silence as they waited for Deuce to arrive at the restaurant where he requested them to meet.

That morning, Silence got a call from Deuce asking for a sit-down. You see, Deuce didn't know what kind of dudes he was dealing with. He figured he'd just come up that way, kill everybody, and go back to Baltimore. But once he saw the gruesome shit these men had no problem doing, he was now reconsidering this whole war thing.

The spot where he wanted to meet was just off the highway, a really busy area with state troopers everywhere; in fact, it was directly across the street from the state troopers barracks. This was smart on his behalf, knowing he'd make it out alive because who would be crazy enough to kill somebody right there. And if they did, the chances of getting away was slim to none.

"We hear what he has to say, and after we handle this, we gotta take care of these other situations out of town. The areas these niggas live in are upscale quiet neighborhoods and I'm feeling them because of the tree lines up and down the blocks . . . It makes it easy for us to blend into the darkness," he replied.

"So we just there for two hits?" Spizz asked.

Spizz was cool but not comfortable with murder, and it especially bothered him sometimes when the families of the victims were involved. Still, he went with it because Silence was his brother and their bond overrode everybody's life.

"Nah, whole houses have to go," he answered calmly as Deuce and Fuego could be seen walking up to where they were sitting in the back of the restaurant.

Fuego was opposed to meeting up with these men. He saw it as pointless and hated that the man who brought him into the game was taking the bitch approach and was about to ask these men for peace. In his mind, Deuce was getting soft and he knew he had to do something about it. For now, he played along because, as it stands, he was the boss, so Fuego stood in line and waited. How much longer, he didn't know, but he did know that peace wasn't an option, especially after the head in the bag shit.

Silence and Spizz had already ordered their food. They arrived an hour before these men had did, so they could check out the places as far as exits and the surrounding area were concerned since it was Deuce who had picked the meeting spot.

"Have a seat," Silence said to the men in between bites of his steak. "So, what's this sit-down all about?" he asked while looking at Deuce's extended hand as if it were a pile of shit.

Silence had never liked peace and anyone asking for it he considered to be weak. He felt that war was necessary and that it balanced out life and life's boundaries—but for amusement's sake, he came to hear this man out.

"You killed my cousin—someone completely innocent in all of this!" replied Deuce through clenched teeth.

"Casualty of war," Silence replied while slicing off another piece of his steak.

Fuego stood behind Deuce, shaking his head, but at the same time he had his hand on his hip, gripping the .40-cal tucked in the waistband.

"This shit has gone too far. What will it take to end this?" asked Deuce as he became more angry.

Spizz and Silence looked at each other, smiling, before Silence answered, "Your life and your life!"

Fuego wanted so badly to end both of these men, but opted against it because of where they were. He knew that if he wanted things to go his own way, he'd have to kill Deuce.

"War you want, then both of you will die and me personally will do this, so enjoy your meals because there will not be too many more," Fuego finally spoke.

Silence laughed and asked the men to kindly remove themselves from their table.

"It's hard for me to enjoy my meal. I mean, I'm like the Italians . . . I only eat with niggas that I fuck with, so please, both of you are excused," he said with a smile.

Deuce locked eyes with Silence. His eyes bloodshot from anger, he thought this meeting would go his way and this war could be put to rest, but now he has to end it by any means.

"I'll see you around," Deuce said as he and Fuego exited their table.

"That went well," Spizz said with a smile.

What those men, including Spizz, didn't know was what came next. Yeah, they chose the meeting spot, but Silence—being the strategist that he was—had bigger plans.

"Yeah, and it's about to get even better, but back to these jobs. Supposedly, one of these cats is heavy on the streets and is fucking up or has fucked up some paper for B-Boy; not quite sure, but I knew you'd be happy to hear that. But we rolling out tomorrow," replied Silence.

"I thought you said you wanted to handle this shit with Deuce before we roll out," Spizz said, slightly confused.

"I did say that and I meant it. We roll out tomorrow," Silence assured his friend. "First we go check up on lil brah and then I have to get with Rican to have him clean shit up while we're gone. I'm pretty sure you have some things to tie up as well."

"What you doin' tonight?" asked Spizz, hoping they could get out and just enjoy one night. I haven't enjoyed myself in a lil minute. All this war shit be stressing me the fuck out, my nigga."

"Take the night and chill, but I have to spend some time with Tish before we roll. She said I've been neglecting her, so I'm taking her out to eat, but don't get too twisted because we roll out in the a.m. I got the cars. Everything is set up. All we have to do is get to each spot," Silence replied. "Now, sit back and enjoy the show because things are about to get pretty interesting."

He smiled to himself, thinking about what was about to happen.

Outside the restaurant

Lynn was outside sitting on a motorcycle as Deuce and Fuego exited the establishment. Neither one of the men paid her any attention as they walked past. They were to focused on the conversation they just had with their enemy.

Lynn was wearing a gray pair of tight-fitting cargo pants with a white halter top and a pair of gray-and-white red bottoms. As she watched the men getting into their vehicle, she put on her helmet and started her chrome-and-white Ducati. The men pulled off and she wasn't too far behind them, always staying at least two cars lengths behind.

She followed the men for quite a few miles and they still hadn't figured out that they were being followed by this beautiful White woman.

Deuce and Fuego were in a deep-sea blue drop-top Challenger, discussing how they would end this war.

"I don't understand why you even wasted your time with that meeting, Deuce. I mean, peace? Are you fucking serious? Them silly-ass niggas killed your fucking cousin, and not just one cousin, but two!" Fuego said in anger as he held up two fingers to show his point. "I don't know what's going on with you, B, but you gotta snap back to reality and get to what we came down here to get. They taking shit to another level, so we should be doing the same, kid."

Deuce was taking everything in and felt real stupid he even considered squashing their beef. He knew what he had to do and he knew how to do it fast, especially if he wanted to stay in power.

"Don't worry about it, and you're right, we just gotta play the game like how they are playing theirs . . . RUTHLESS! The kid Rozay, he's still at the hospital and I understand he might be there for a while, so he's sitting duck and an easy target. So get someone down there and have them cut his head off like they did to Zelda. After that . . . anyone close to them, women, children, and whoever else, cut their heads off as well. And each one I want them delivered the same way Zelda's was," Deuce replied.

The men made an exit off of the highway and headed into the town where they resided. As they approached a red light on a corner just a block away from where they were going, Lynn pulled up on the side of them and lifted the face up her helmet.

"Hey there, Deucey. In case you're wondering, Silence sent me . . . He had a message for you," Lynn said while pulling out a Glock 19 she had in a fanny pack around her waist. "He said, 'Check mate!'" she continued as she emptied the clip into him and Fuego.

Lynn U-turned her bike and peeled out in the opposite direction, smiling as if she won the lottery.

CHAPTER

26

That night, Silence took Tish to a romantic little getaway. Before he got with her, he met up with Rozay and told him to finish off the rest of Deuce's crew. From there, he picked up Tish and took her on a shopping spree. She loved every minute with her man, especially since she didn't get much time with him to begin with, so every moment was precious to her.

Silence took Tish on a boat ride to have dinner. He had the whole thing set up—a private chef, candles all around the yacht's dining area, and her favorite song playing through the boat's speakers. They were docked right along the city coastline, giving them the most amazingly beautiful view of the casino lights.

He was dressed to impress as well, wearing a two-piece gray Armani suit and shoes. Tish was wearing a white Gucci dress with matching shoes and she was as icy as she wanted to be.

"Here . . . take these," Silence said as he handed Tish a pair of binoculars.

"What am I supposed to do with these?" she asked, slightly confused.

"Look towards the Tropicana. You should see a few baby-blue screens . . . you know . . . you favorite color," Silence replied with a smile.

Tish took the binoculars and began to scan the coastline towards the casino. As she found the blue screens lit up around the casino, she focused the binoculars more so that she could read what the screens said.

Tish began to shake uncontrollably as she read the words: *Latisha Rose, WILL YOU MARRY ME? Saying yes would truly make my life complete.*

When she finally turned around, Silence was in front of her on one knee, holding the biggest ring she had ever seen, seven carats to be exact.

"Oh my god . . . Yes, I will marry you. And what took you so long?" she asked while still crying.

Silence smiled and kissed her on her forehead before responding. "No time like the present, and I asked myself that same question . . . What's taking so long? You understand my love for you and that love increases by the day. You are the mother of my child and you are a true reflection of me. You're my queen, my every dream, and truly my everything and I know that I don't express these feelings to you that often, but never think anything different than what I am telling you right at this very moment," he replied as Tish began to cry even more. "Have I ever told you how sexy you are when you cry?" he said with a smile.

Tish smiled back and playfully punched Silence on the arm, saying it was his fault the tears were there in the first place.

"Tears of joy though, and I promise you nothing but happiness for the rest of our lives," Silence continued. "Come! Let's eat," he said as he pulled her towards the table that was set up for them.

"Are you staying with me tonight?" she asked, hopeful that he'd say yes.

"Of course, and we are staying here, right on this boat."

"This is beautiful, Silence, and I want you to know how much I truly appreciate you. Every day I cry just hoping nothing will happen to you. Even though you don't talk about it, I know what it is that you do out on those streets. I don't like it, but this is what I accepted because that is something you would have to do yourself, but know that I accept everything about you; the good, the bad, and the ugly, and I will always ride for you and with you . . . to the moon and back," Tish said with tears in her eyes.

"And this is why I want you as my wife," he replied.

Silence knew Tish was a rider and he trusted that she would always remain silent when it came to him. On top of that, he truly did love and would do anything but give up the game for her.

Murder was and still is his first love, and he will never stop the way he feeds his family, or at least that what he thought.

"After tonight I will be out of town for the next few days, maybe a week, tops, but I will definitely keep you posted as far as my movements and time," he said, knowing his wife-to-be would be understanding.

"Okay, but please come back to me," she pleaded.

"I'll always come back to you," he replied.

Around the hood

Rozay signed himself out of the hospital against the doctors' orders. He and Rican sat on a stoop, talking about what was next. Rozay had to walk with crutches and of course had his shit bag, so it would be hard for him to put in any work at the moment, but let him tell it, his trigger finger was still good.

"That shit-crazy kid, a White girl on a bike killed these niggas! She did what we couldn't do and that's deep. I wonder who the fuck she was. I mean, I know that brah set that shit up, but who the fuck is the bitch?" Rozay questioned.

"You know he been having Lynn around him lately, and you know she was always on some solo quiet shit all in her own head, so I guess brah saw something in her. It was a good hit though, clean and fast, just like Si likes it," Rican said, smiling and wishing he could have been there to see their faces when a White bitch was sent to kill them. Crazy, right?

"Word, I fucks with shorty. But what about the rest of them cats? I mean, I know they big homie dead, but they still going try and get back over this shit," Rozay said with concern in his voice.

"Si told me to finish this thing up and that's what I'll do. You're out of commission for a minute, so you handle the money aspect and I'll get a few lil homies to go finish the rest of them bean-eating ass goyas," Rican replied.

"So how we going do this?" asked Rozay, wanting to know all the details.

"One at a time," Rican said with a sinister smile.

A few days prior, Muhmit came up with the locations of where Deuce and his team were staying, so the plan was to hit 'em in the middle of the night when no one would expect it.

"Spizz and Si are going out of town tomorrow, so we gone hit 'em then," Rican said as he lit a blunt. "But you, we got 1,500 bricks to move and we gotta move 'em quick. Shit been hot out here and flow haven't been coming through because of the fear of getting hot. Spizz said, for now, drop the price to $85 a brick. I got some Bridgeton cats coming through for 300 of those and you can give Champ and Bone 200 a piece and let them niggas know that they got forty-eight hours to get rid of them."

"We got shooters on every corner, on all three blocks, so them niggas won't catch us slipping ever again. And after this shit is over, Spizz told me we gotta patch shit up in this city. He want niggas to come together and focus on getting this money. Niggas come to Atlantic City, they gotta see us, we gotta grow this shit, my nigga. You know, push niggas out of town out of the way. If you ain't getting it from us and you moving it, you die—simple as that," Rican said while passing the blunt to Rozay.

"Word, I'm with the shit, but who gone arrange this sit-down with these niggas?" Rozay asked.

Rican sat there in a daze, thinking about the future of this family, and now he was focused more than ever. Yeah, Spizz and Si were big brahs, but he had as much respect in the hood as they did and with their guidance what he and his squad could accomplish would be endless.

"The boss of all bosses. You know niggas don't see 'em too often, but when he makes a call, niggas respect it . . . Silence gone set it up and we gone be there. Imagine this city coming together on the money tip? Fuck New York, fuck Philly. . . WE THE COAST!" Rican answered.

"I like that. Money is the motive and we gotta get it, and if you ain't getting money, then I can't stand next to you . . . Squad shit, FAMILY NIGGA!" Rozay replied.

"So what's the plan for tonight? I know we not just gone sit around here doing nothing?" Rozay said in a joking yet serious matter.

"Nah, Spizz wanted to go out as well. He hit me earlier saying he needed a break from all this shit and wanted to chill before him and Si took their trip. He said something about Mur Mur over at the Bogata. They having some kind of after-party. You know, Nicki Minaj having a concert at the Bogata right now as we speak and the after-party is for her, so brah wanted to slide through," Rican replied.

"Yeah, we there, but I gotta go get dressed. It's eight-forty now, so I'll be ready by ten and we can swing through, cripple and all," Rozay joked.

"Say less. I'ma drop you off at ya spot and when you ready, just hit me so I can come back and get you.

"What's up with Si? He coming out with us or what? We kicked earlier about the situation, but he never said whether or not he had plans for the rest of the night?" Rican said.

"Nah, Si is occupied for the night. He said he was spending time with Tish before their trip and he is supposed to be proposing, and they out on a mini yacht somewhere. That's the first time I ever saw brah smile when he told me about the proposal," said Rozay.

"Word, that's good for Si. I respect that. But we gotta go, so bring ya crippled ass on and don't be spilling that shit bag in my truck!" Rican joked as the men walked to his car. "Tomorrow, its right back to business!" he added.

CHAPTER

27

It was business as usual around the projects. The hustling and bustling of the early morning dope friends, young boys securing the blocks while the older heads ran the dope spots. The fire with the fuzz died down a little, just enough for the family to eat, and Rozay took full advantage of that. It wasn't even halfway through the morning and they were already down to about 600 bricks.

A few O.T. niggas came through and gripped some work. and the ground flow was jumping due to the price decrease. Rican was somewhere with a few young goons planning the hit for the night while Silence and Spizz were on their way to whatever it was they were headed, so for that day Rozay was the face and head of the operation.

He sat parked in a wheelchair in the middle of the hood to monitor progress alongside another cat he grew up with named Moose. Moose had just come home that morning. He did a little stretch for a robbery a few years back and couldn't wait to jump head first into the family business.

"Damn, kid, when can I get into position? That shit running like a corporate structure. You got the security, the collectors, and the trappers," Moose said while motioning his hands in a dramatic fashion.

Moose was never really a get-money nigga. He was more so the kick-in-ya-door type . . . Never nothing big, just small shit, you know, a few bands here, a couple there, so Rozay was hesitant to even consider putting any work in his hands.

"You just got out not even two hours ago, my G. Chill regular and let ya situation play out. Besides, it's not up to me . . . You gotta holla at Rican or Spizz about that," Rozay said as he hit the blunt one more time before passing it to Moose.

"Damn, all this time you been out here outing in work and you ain't got no say-so around these parts?" Moose responded slightly sarcastic.

"Watch ya mouth. It's different niggas for different jobs, and I'm comfortable in my own position. With thoughts like that . . . you'll dig ya own grave, LITERALLY!" said Rozay in a more than serious tone.

"I was just fucking with you, my nigga. I ain't mean no harm by that," he replied, seeing how uneasy it made Rozay.

"Well, I don't play games. I tend to stop 'em before they begin. Do ya self a favor . . . don't talk like that around my niggas; they the real zero-tolerance type," said Rozay, locking eyes with his childhood friend to show him how serious shit was with his family.

Moose grew up around the projects, but he wasn't really around certain cats growing up. Yeah people knew who he was, but he wasn't quite as welcomed as everybody else.

"You got it, my G. So when can I holla at Rican or Spizz? 'Cause I'm trying to get to it. I been down for too long and I can't be out this bitch fucked up, you feel me?" asked Moose.

Before Rozay could say anything else, several shots could be heard on the next block over along with a few loud screens.

"Y'all niggas, go check that shit out!" Rozay yelled to a couple of young boys posted outside a nearby trap house.

As the youngins ran off in the direction where the shots rang off, Moose pushed Rozay in the wheelchair as fast as he could without tipping him over.

As the men all approached the block, three bodies could be seen lying on the side of a porch a few feet away from the stop sign. Just across the street, another body was laid out next to a car that had crashed into a pole.

Upon further inspection, Rozay saw it was a young boy by the name of Live that he had patrolling that area in case them boarder cats came through. Next to him were two little kids—a boy and a girl—with gunshot wounds to the chest and face. On top of the sirens, women could be heard screaming as they ran up the block to the crime scene.

"Yo, grab that strap right there," Rozay told Moose while pointing at the gun lying next to Live's dead body. "Go get rid of it before them boys pull up," he further instructed. He then asked another youngin posted to that same corner, "Ayo, Dolla. What happened, kid?"

"Man, that car right there came up and two niggas hopped out shooting. I and Live started throwing shots back. Live saw two kids by the porch slouched down and ran over to shield them, but it was too late. The second shooter ran that way," he replied pointing in the opposite direction of the crashed car.

The crowd on the block began to grow as police and ambulance swarmed the area. Officers began pushing the crowd back to make a perimeter around the bodies, while homicide detectives started to examine the crime scene.

"Aight, get outta here and stay low until I call you. And don't talk to nobody else. Go straight to your crib!" Rozay said as he himself wheeled his chair in the opposite direction.

On the other side of town

Rican had brought two dudes from out of town for the hit that night and they were in an abandoned house on the west side of the city, loading their weapons.

Star and Kane were these two crazy-ass cats from Newark he met during a juvenile bid. They got fly over time because of how thorough Rican was. These two men were Eastside, a blood set on the East Coast; in the prison system, they tried to dominate the jails and this was no exception for Rican.

When they tried to test him over the TV in the dayroom, he proved he was one not to fold. Every day for two weeks either he fought or got jumped by these men. After a while they saw how real he was and eventually asked him to join their ranks. Of course Rican opted against that and after a while the men became close to him, occasionally putting in work for the other once they were released.

"YO, I just got a text from my right hand . . . Them niggas just went around my way shooting. They killed one of my young boys and two little kids. He said two shooters came and one got away. I'm thinking about saying fuck tonight and go out there now 'cause these niggas just don't know when the war is lost," said Rican, showing complete aggression in his movements.

"Nah, kid, we gotta stick to the script. You can't act off emotions 'cause that shit will jam us all up. We play it how it's planned; you go your way and we'll go ours. Now, you sure that everyone will be at this one spot?" Star asked, wanting to make sure that the hit went well and they didn't miss any of their targets.

Rican got wind of the spot they were occupying and planned on hitting both the front and back doors at the same time, killing everybody inside. At least six more of those dudes who came from Baltimore with Deuce were staying there, at least that is what these men were told. Accurate or not, they knew what had to be done and, that night, whoever occupied that crib was sure to die.

"Yeah, that's the location I got. I scoped it out a few times and did indeed see a few of them niggas in and out, so we'll hit 'em at about three in the a.m.," Rican replied.

"Then that's what it is. But you know that favor we talked about for this hit right?" asked Kane.

Of course nothing is free and deeds must always be compensated, so the men discussed some sort payment to be paid after the job was complete. When Rican asked what the price would be, the neb said none was needed, just another act of appreciation.

"Yeah, so what's the damage?" replied Rican.

"An introduction to the plug," both men responded in unison.

"Aight, cool. I'll set it up with my big brah," he answered.

Both Kane and Star looked at each other slightly confused, not knowing if they heard what it was that Rican said correctly.

"Nah, we mean the plug, plug. I know you niggas is getting money, but I don't think that y'all could handle the kind of work we looking for," Star explained.

Rican laughed a little before answering simply. "He *is* the plug!"

Back around the hood . . .

Rozay and Moose were sitting on a wall that divided each block, talking about what had just happened. For Rozay this was just another violence-filled day, but for Moose he was a little thrown off by what he had just seen.

"Damn, brah. I mean, I heard about the beef y'all had, but through broad daylight shooting and hitting kids and shit. These dudes are disrespectful on another level, my G. So what we doing about this situation?" Moose asked with a sense of urgency in his voice.

Rozay was zoned and didn't answer right away. He wanted so desperately to be there when the work was being put in and hated that he let them bean-eating ass goyas catch him slipping like that. For now there was nothing he could do but let the situation play out, no matter how bad he wanted to get his own revenge.

"We do nothing . . . It's being handled and know that—being around us—you ask no questions. Like I told you, it's different niggas for different jobs and right now your only job is to play ya position and not focus so much on what is taking place around. You just came home and trying to jump into a beef that has little to do with you. Focus on what you want to do to better ya situation and from there . . . we talk."

Later that night . . .

Rican and Star were at the front of the house where Deuce's men were said to be staying. Kane was at the back door, waiting for them to let him in. The house looked to be pretty dark with the exception of a few rooms lit up from the TVs. It was a two-story home at the end of a dead-end block on the south side of the Ville.

The other houses on the block were pretty rundown and it looked more like a trap block than anything else, but there was no activity in sight. After careful inspection of the lower level, making sure no one was visible, Star began to pick the lock and let themselves in.

Rican went to the back to let Kane in when a downstairs door could be heard screeching open.

The three men locked eyes in the darkness and all began firing in that direction. Screams could be heard upstairs as the men continued towards the stairs. They reached the steps there was a figure at the top, so they began to fire again but not before Star got hit and knocked into the wall by a shotgun blast.

"YOU GOOD?" Kane yelled to his friend.

"Yeah. It was pellets. Most of 'em hit the vest . . . I'm good, though," Star replied as Kane helped him up while Rican continued to fire.

Once all the men were upstairs, they began to sweep each room, killing three more men. At the other end of the hall, someone began to fire shots through one of the bedroom doors, hitting Rican in the back of his leg. All three men turned around and fired shots through the door until all of their clips were empty.

The men stood there listening for movement while they loaded another clip into their weapons. Satisfied, they pushed towards the back of the house, and when they saw that everyone there was dead, the men ran out of the house to their waiting getaway car.

CHAPTER
28

Silence and Spizz had just arrived in Elizabeth to pay a visit to Maurice, one of the cats that B-Boy wanted hit. They were sitting in a car parked across the street form Maurice's three-story home in the suburban section of the city. Both men were dressed in all black and armed with P89s, with silencers attached.

It was about twelve midnight and neighborhood watch had just made their rounds for the third time in the last hour. One set of patrols were made by an unmarked police car, which seemed to come through every hour on the hour; the other two by the good citizens of the neighborhood.

"So when are we going in? We been waiting here for two hours now," asked Spizz, growing impatient, as always.

"Now!" answered Silence as he watched the lady walking her dog hit the corner.

The men crept across the street, hiding in the shadows along the tree line that occupied each side of the block. Maurice had two Great Danes in his front yard. As the men approached, so did these two beasts of a dog.

Both Silence and Spizz fired a single shot into each of the dogs' heads and proceeded over the 10-foot-high cast-iron gate. As the men entered the front yard of the property, the motion sensors caused the yard to light up with bright LED lights. The men made it to the side of the house and waited a few minutes until the light went off automatically. They shot the sensors.

Silence walked along the sides of the property to disarm the alarm system. Once that was done, both men proceeded to the backyard to find a way into the two-story home.

Spizz looked around the property in hopes of finding an open or unlocked window while Silence worked on trying to get the back sliding doors open.

The house was pretty quiet and extremely dark, with the exception of a dim light that came from an upstairs bedroom.

"We in!" Silence whispered low enough to where he couldn't be heard from afar, but loud enough for Spizz to hear from where he was standing, about fifteen feet away.

"You already know what it is. Once we're in, we separate and kill everyone you see . . . But save the target for me!" Silence continued to whisper.

They entered the sliding door that led into the kitchen/dining area. The house had an open floor plan, making it easy for both men to navigate through the darkness of the first level of Maurice's home.

"Down here is clear, bruh. I don't think nobody is even here," Spizz whispered.

Silence nodded for Spizz to go upstairs with him to be sure that the house was indeed empty.

The men cleared each room upon reaching the top of the stairs. The house remained silent with no sign of life, but there was still one room towards the back of the house that the men haven't yet gotten to.

"One more room," Silence pointed.

He and Spizz slowly approached the room at the end of the hall.

There was a little light coming under the door, apparently from a TV, due to the flickering and different colorations reflecting on the shiny waxed floor that ran throughout the home.

The men looked at each other. Silence opened the door a crack and peeked in to find Maurice sleeping alone with a blanket covering only the bottom half of his body.

The men entered, each of them standing on the opposite side of the sleeping man's bed. He must have felt their presence because he woke up and in one motion reached for a gun he had under his pillow.

"Not so fast," Spizz said as he cracked him on the side of his head with his gun.

The man cried out in pain and asked what the two men wanted.

"For someone who seems to piss people off, you sure do have very light security," Silence said sarcastically, completely ignoring the man's question.

"Where's the money?" Spizz asked, getting straight to the point.

"It's in a safe in the back of the closet!" the man said while still holding the side of his head as blood gushed out.

"Well, get up and get it!" Spizz continued with a smile.

The man crawled out of the bed and led the way to the closet across the room. Opening the door, he moved a few clothes out of the way and proceeded to punch the combination into the key code on the front of the safe.

As the safe door began to open, Silence put two bullets into the back of Maurice's head.

"What the fuck, my nigga. I wasn't done with 'em yet!" Spizz said angrily while stepping over the body to empty the contents of the safe.

"I was!" Silence shot back. "Now hurry up so we can go get this other shit over with," he continued.

After collecting the money, the men exited the home following the same route in which they entered and proceeded back to their vehicle and went on their way.

"Next stop . . . Hoboken!" Silence said as they drove away from the property.

Meanwhile, back home

Rozay, Danny, and Sudan were in the middle of counting money when the front door of the trap house they were at got kicked in by SWAT and what seemed to be the whole Atlantic City police force.

Sudan had just came home that morning from a little Fed stretch for money laundering and happened to fall right into the hands of someone else's indictment, or so it seemed. Neither of them expected this event to have taken place due to the countless youngins paid to keep track of the corners in case of situations like these. But that day, no warning came and these men were caught slipping.

Rican happened to be O.T. handling things in the next county over; in fact, he had just left about an hour before the raid.

"NOBODY FUCKING MOVE!" the police yelled as they waved their assault rifles around the room, moving about and making sure everyone was secure.

"What the FUCCCKKK?" Rozay yelled out to no one in particular.

He couldn't believe this was happening, at least not now. They had just got back control of the streets and pretty much just ended the war—*and now this?* he thought as he lay down, his life flashing before his eyes.

Not only was he still injured, but he had a baby on the way that he has been keeping to himself and away from his family. He didn't hide her out of embarrassment; it was more so for her protection, and the truth would soon come out as to who this woman truly was.

Rozay met Cymone about a year-and-a-half before the raid. He bumped into her on The Walk, a shopping area along the city. Cymone looked to be Asian of some sort, probably Cambodian, and looked to be part, if not half, White. Shorty was beautiful . . . around 5'3", nice and petite with a short little pixie cut, the one that Rihanna rocks. She was fly though, a little street-smart but on a highly educated level. From what Rozay knew, she had moved to Jersey from Ohio for a job after she graduated from college, majoring in finance.

Something was always off about her, but Rozay was blinded by her beauty so couldn't see it.

"Roger Lewis . . . We have warrants and you are under arrest for Rico-influenced crimes, money laundering, and attempted murder of a federal witness," the officer said as he cuffed Rozay's hands behind his back.

"Attempted what? What the fuck y'all talking about? I ain't attempt to do shit, all that y'all got on me is all of this fucking money. Y'all faggot-ass cops is tripping!" he raged as foam started to appear around his mouth.

"Yo, chill brah. You gone be good!" yelled Sudan from across the room. "Trust that."

Rozay knew better than to keep work in the spot with the money, so all that there was for the cops to take were a couple of guns and a few hundred thousand.

If only the alphabet boys knew . . . all of the work was right next door in an upstairs unit of a friend's crib.

But the question still remained, *how the fuck did this whole shit even happened?*

As the men were escorted out of the complex in cuffs, Rozay noticed black SUVs parked all around the projects; there were police everywhere and it seemed as if every young boy that was paid to watch the blocks were lined up and down the street, cuffed and sitting along the sidewalk.

"How did we not see this shit coming?" Rozay continued asking himself while being put into the back of one of the waiting SUVs.

Everything was about to fall apart on all fronts and Rican would be the one left alone to gather the pieces.

"MOOSE!" Rozay thought out loud as he watched the hood unravel from the back seat of the vehicle.

Moose had been missing in action since the day Rozay got hit up. I mean, yeah, he came around, but it was always for a few minutes at a time.

In fact, the last time Rozay saw Moose, he was with Cymone, and Moose was with some White chick; they bumped into each other at his hibachi spot outside of the city.

When Rozay introduced Cymone to him, it seemed as if they were already familiar with each other like they knew one another, but Rozay brushed it off, thinking maybe he was tripping.

Pieces were staring to come together in his mind, but was he right?

Or were the cuffs playing tricks on him? Either way, things would come to light.

CHAPTER

29

Silence and Spizz arrived in Hoboken just a few hours later and were now outside of the next target's home. It was a townhouse in a suburban area on the east side of the city. The men had already switched their vehicles and stashed the money from the last hit in a nearby hotel room, where another vehicle was waiting once this job was complete.

"You ready?" Silence asked Spizz as he noticed him looking up and down the block in search of nosey neighbors.

"Yeah, but this time, let me get everything before you go all gun-happy," he joked as they both pulled mask over their faces.

This street, like Maurice's, was extremely quiet with the exception of a few dogs barking in the distance.

The men crept along the tree line to the side and then to the back of the property.

The house was pretty easy to get into, especially since the back door was unlocked.

Noise, along with flickering lights, could be heard coming from the room just outside of the kitchen. The men knew the family was home because of the minivan parked in front of the garage, as well as the lights that shone through every other window around the house. The rest of the block was pretty dark.

"It seems they are in the living room watching a movie. Son ain't here, though," whispered Silence as they made their way through the sliding door. "You go left and creep up behind them and I'll get 'em straight on," he continued while pointing Spizz in the direction of the laundry next to the kitchen, which also led around to the home's living room.

The victim's wife was on the love seat, holding a little girl while watching the movie *Shrek*. Right next to them sat a young man, maybe in his late teens to early twenties, sitting in a recliner and texting on his phone.

None of them were aware of the men in their home and what was about to happen.

Spizz crept up behind the love seat, which was facing the other side of the room. As he approached, the young kid saw his reflection and jumped out of his seat in pure terror. Before he could scream or react, Silence stepped from beyond the darkness into the light.

"Nobody move. Cooperate and maybe—just maybe—you all will live," Silence said as Spizz approached the family, zip ties in hand.

"Please don't hurt my babies!" the woman came to cry as she was the first to be tied up.

"You married the wrong man," Silence said as he shushed her with a smile.

He kept his gun aimed at the boy until Spizz tied him up. Once they all were subdued, he sat on the edge of the table in front of the man's wife and simply asked.

"When will he be home? Can't speak, huh? Guess you're useless," said Silence as he opened the duffel bag he carried with him and pulled out a small machete.

"One more time . . . when?"

Before the woman got the chance to answer, he swung the machete with the quickness of a samurai onto the left side of her neck, almost severing her head completely.

The little girl began to scream, so Spizz grabbed the blanket they were wrapped in and stuffed the end of it into the little girl's mouth.

Silence then swung the machete again, this time causing the woman's head to fall to the ground as blood squirted out of the top of her neck; her body sat up for a second before sliding off the edge of the love seat.

Silence then sat on the edge of the living room table and began rolling a blunt as Spizz walked over to the front window to wait on their next target.

Meanwhile in A.C.

Rican had just arrived back into the city and had heard of what took place during his absence. The first thing he did was call the team's lawyer to let him know what was going on and also to find out if there were warrants out for him as well.

Things were going so good up until this point and this was now another bump in the road, a bump that soon will be revealed that could have been avoided.

Once he found out that there weren't any warrants, he tried desperately to call Spizz and Silence to let them know what had happened, but he couldn't reach either of them.

"What the fuck!" he yelled while banging on the steering wheel of his car.

This put a major dent in their operation and on top of that, his best friend, his brother, and his crutch just got bagged and now he was the only one left—it seemed like he had no one. As he continued talking to himself about what was going on, Fresh pulled up beside him to ask if there was anything he could help him with until shit got figured out.

"Right now, brah, I don't know . . . I don't know where none of the work is that was around here or whether or not the shit got caught up in the raid. I can't reach the bros and the hood is too hot for me to even go around to check up on things," Rican replied. "I'ma get with you later. I gotta check on something!" he added as he sped off with too much on his mind.

Back in Hoboken

"Tick . . . tock!" Silence repeated as he pointed his gun from the son to the daughter, taunting them both.

The man they were waiting for finally came home, but not before Silence killed his son, who was just home on Christmas break.

"About time this nigga came the fuck home. I was tired of waiting here," said the always impatient Spizz.

As the man entered his home, he was surprised by what he saw. There lay his wife's lifeless body with her head cut off and his son slumped in the corner with bullet holes in his head and chest.

He knew these men were after money, but couldn't understand why they would kill his family like this, especially to this extent.

He tried the tough guy roll of not giving it up, saying he was going to die anyway so why bother, but in hopes of these men letting his daughter live . . . he gave up everything, still to have his baby girl shot to death. All up at the end.

That night, he died twice—once when he watched his only daughter murdered in front of him and then when he took shots to the head himself.

As the men gathered the bags to leave, Silence got a funny feeling in the pit of his stomach but disregarded it as nothing.

"Next stop . . . B-Boy!" Silence said as they discussed what was next.

As the men hit the corner, they were surrounded by black SUVs and men demanding them to shut the car off and step out with their hands in the air.

After Silence and Spizz were taken into custody, they learned that the men they killed were working with the Feds to bring B-Boy down. That last victim of the night was being watched by local narcotics and that B-Boy was well aware of this information. This was why he used Silence instead of his own men to do the hit.

He figured that without these two informants, they wouldn't have anything on him and he also knew Silence, being the standup nigga that he was, wouldn't consider bringing him down for ordering the hits.

Silence and Spizz were charged with first-degree murder as well as five other counts of murder, false imprisonment, along with several weapons charges.

They fought their case for three years and ended up losing trial on felony murder; both received a sentence of 185 years. For years from behind the wall, these men have been in search of B-Boy.

After the smoke cleared, B-Boy got wind that Silence and Spizz had a lot of money on his head and cats from all over wanted the bounty. B-boy failed to realize how much love Silence had all over, even in his hood, so nobody had seen or heard from him since . . . up until now.

Present day, Trenton State Prison

Silence continued thinking back to the night of the murders and how he met B-Boy. For years, he had regretted breaking his own rules—if only he could have changed the outcome. The years they were gone, they still had a strong hold on the streets and Rican made sure of that.

Rozay was out on bail, still fighting his case, and things were beginning to unfold.

Amanda and Jessica still played a major part in the team and product was still plentiful.

Rican had his resources all of the coast and as far south as Alabama in search of B-Boy. Finally he found a break and couldn't wait to send word to his family.

Spizz sat and watched as the wheels turned in his brother's head. He knew getting B-Boy was the next best thing behind fighting for their appeal.

"Where is he?" Silence finally said.

"Greensboro, South Carolina!" replied Spizz.

Silence sat with a smile on his face, knowing B-Boy's days were numbered and he'd finally get his revenge.

"Tell Rican to send Lynn to me. Tell him to tell her that it is urgent that I see her this weekend!" Silence said with a sinister smile.

The End

. . . at least 'til next time.

A TRILOGY

In the words of Juelz Santana, I told this story because I wanted to let people know how real shit really is. I mean, people will always try to get one over you, but *Protect What's Yours*, *Protect Your Family*, and *Protect What's Right*!

Book 2 coming soon: **"Protect Your Family: Operation Broken Glass"**

I would like to stress that this book is a work of fiction and any similarities are simply coincidental.